GRAVE MATTERS

BY CARLOTTA G. HOLTON

Dorrance Publishing Co
701 Smithfield Street
Pittsburgh, PA 15222
Visit our website at *www.dorrancebookstore.com*

ISBN: 978-1-4809-1115-4
eISBN 978-1-4809-1437-7

"When the human race has once acquired a superstition, nothing short of death is ever likely to remove it."

Mark Twain

TABLE OF CONTENTS

INTRODUCTION
LILLY'S LAW

"In the province of the mind, what is believed to be true is true or becomes true, within certain limits to be found experientially and experimentally. These limits are further beliefs to be transcended. In the province of the mind, there are no limits."

Dr. John C. Lilly, *The Center of the Cyclone*

When I wrote the collection of short stories based on superstitions, *Touching the Dead,* I realized that I had uncovered a Pandora's chest filled with potential stories that would take the reader on many more armchair journeys. As I have traveled and continued to research and explore this unchartered territory of the mind, my own belief that we are governed by these superstitions has strengthened. Some do not act upon these beliefs, others for whom these superstitions have a psychological control, may be influenced to act accordingly upon them – just in case.

To those skeptics, I say: We cling to our superstitions in the face of reason. Only one event, coincidence or experience can make a convert. Some say that science can sweep away the cobwebs of superstitions. If this is true, then why do some of us still believe? What do you think?

OTHER BOOKS

Salem Pact

Touching the Dead

Honorable Mention, 2011 Beach Book Festival
Best Anthology/Compilation 2008- New England Book Festival
Best Horror Book of the Year 2007- Booksandauthors.net
2nd Place Best Fiction Award Books at Large National Federation of Press Women

Vampire Resurrection

Third Place Best Fiction, National Federation of Press Women
First Place New Jersey Press Women 2009
Finalist, Fiction, Horror National Best Books 2009 Awards, USA Book News

Deadly Innocence

Honorable Mention Fiction, Halloween Book Festival, 2012

SAVING FACE

"... Human superstitions die hard. The heads thereof may be cut off, but their noxious bodies of suspicions writher long."

Mary Wilkins Freeman, *The Witch's Daughter*

There is a decided aura of mystery that envelops Venice. It is an invisible gauze that, unbeknownst to its visitors, casts its netting around the city, especially in the evening beneath the watchful eye of the moon. While lovers drink in the romance of a gondola ride, it is merely a façade of what goes on here. Beware to the ignorant who dare to traverse the darkened alleys connected by bridges which span the maze of canals. Those who have lost their way can tell you there is an inexplicable force that erupts through the membrane of time, like heat waves writhing from a pavement on a sultry day, confronting the unsuspecting traveler. People have gone missing here.

Alongside the shops brimming with colorfully decorated glittering masks, there are some who claim there is darkness here beneath the surface that waits to capture the attention. They whisper of battles between angels and demons, strange suicides, and murders inside of centuries-old palazzos. And of course, ghosts.

There are legends about Ca' Dario, a palace on the Grand Canal with a long history of murder and suicide. The "Dario curse," as it is called, has caused the highest number of deaths of all the other palaces. And it's not just the past that has claimed victims here. Bass guitarist John Entwistle of The Who was renting this palace at the time of his death in 2002.

Tourists are often taken to the Bridge of Sighs, which passes over the Rio di Palazzo, connecting the New Prison to the interrogation rooms in the Doge's Palace. It was the last view of Venice that convicts saw before their imprisonment. Named by Lord Byron in the 19th century, it suggested the prisoners would sigh at their final view of the city through the window before being taken down to their cells. It is a legend, since the days of inquisitions and executions were over by the time the bridge was built in 1602, and the cells under the palace roof were occupied mostly by small-time convicts. However, many still insist the sighs of the prisoners can still be heard.

They do not bury the dead here. It is simply not feasible. One cannot dig more than a few feet without hitting water. So the nearby island of San Michele – a five minute waterbus ride away – houses the dead of Venice. The grand architectural gate and walls give the illusion of a floating fortress. Hundreds of thousands of bodies rest in this semi-circle of mausoleums. Of course, those whose bodies have never been recovered, are but some of the restless spirits that malinger the streets of the city; and from the stories that have been told, their numbers are many. Hauntings are spoken of quite frequently. The Bridge of Sighs attracts many tourists, where they are told of the stories of those incarcerated; the imprisoned who yearned for their freedom and eventually died within the walls.

Venice is a capsule in time. This illusion is presided over by the ornate St. Mark's Basilica, and the seemingly innocuous bell tower that metes out the time before the damp decay of centuries of water slapping against ancient buildings inevitably claims it for its own. Inhabitants are very much aware of this symbiotic relationship and realize that nature is biding its time.

This floating city is always a site of contrasts, but more so during the celebration of its pre-Lenten Carnivale season. It is a time of magic, and some of it rests upon the wearing of *masca,* masks. The festival celebrates the passage from winter into spring; a time when it is considered anything is possible, including the belief that even the humble can become powerful by wearing a mask. The mask, it is believed, invests the wearer with the traits of its persona.

Begun in 1296, the Venice Carnival was designated a public holiday. After an interruption lasting almost two hundred years, it was reinstated in 1980. For many Italians born here, superstitions die hard. Such is the case with Signor Antonio De Faruci, a wealthy businessman who makes his home in a medieval castle in Tuscany. This year, as for the past ten, he has rented out one of the old palazzos on the Grand Canal. As his valet unpacks his things, he makes his way to the San Paolo district to a little "mask lab" near the Rialto Bridge. He is there to pick up two very special masks, on the outside, examples of characters from the Commedia dell'Arte, traced back to the 16th century form of improvisational theatre. The designers of these masks are artistic masters capable of working in various mediums. He marvels at the creations. Traditional masks can be made in leather or with the original design using papiermache, but this special shop uses special materials, applied with gesso and gold leaf, all hand-painted using feathers and gems.

He returns in time with his treasures and puts on his costume: Dottore Peste, or the plague doctor. He slowly buttons the long black coat and high leather boots. The hat is next. The grotesque mask with its abnormally long proboscis, sits on the bed.

Meanwhile, the waterways are teeming, filled with water taxis churning the normally calm waters of the sea as they carry their costumed characters to the event of the year. The setting sun bleeds orange across the vast sky, highlighting the Romanesque, Renaissance, and Gothic architecture of this city of merchants.

As they disembark and find their way to the palazzo, each guest puts on their finishing touch to their costumes. The weight and sheer volume of some of the masks are such that they make walking any distance difficult. Venice is not the only society that has perpetuated the use of masks for their galas. Every culture has hidden behind masks. Their purpose is to conceal the true identity of the wearer. Here in this city, the masks were taken on during the plague, and the characters are very traditional. It is the hope of many that the mask transforms them, if only for the night.

The host wears the mask of the Dottore, or Doctor. He is recognized by his long nose, which supposedly at the time carried garlic to ward off the plague. While everyone comes with a mask, he has especially designed two for some very important guests who will undoubtedly find their unveiling at midnight with a surprise.

"Buono noche," Dottore Pesce greets the young woman he knows as Francesca. Her exquisite figure is enhanced by a shimmering green gown, which shows off a faux diamond necklace, complemented with chandelier earrings made more beautiful by the gentle curve of her ear. Soft tendrils swirl around her face, while the bulk of her blond hair is piled high upon her head. Her Dama mask is covered in jewels.

"Signor."

"Ah, it is Francesca." She curtsies.

He offers her his arm and they walk over to a table lit with candelabras. The room is aglow. The Murano crystal chandelier sends off glittering light, reflected in the cream marbled floors. The melodic strains of a violin set the tone. Perched on a table sit two velvet bags. Dottore reaches for the red one and presents it to his guest.

"I know you are wearing a mask, and a lovely one it is, but as a special favor to me, I would like you to wear this one instead." He holds up the red velvet bag for her to see, but does not open it.

"I had it designed especially for you, and the gems which decorate it are real. I assure you. When you leave tonight, you most certainly keep it as a remembrance." Her present disguise is exquisite, and she has no clue as to what this one looked like.

She squirms with annoyance and crinkles her nose, so as to slightly alter the placement of the mask she is already wearing.

"I don't know. May I see it and then decide?"

"No. You must take it in good faith. Do you not trust me?"

For a woman such as she, who had been unfaithful, it is a bold taunt.

He continues, "It suits you, my dear. It brings out the real you." He continues to hold out the bag, and finally she concedes. *After all,* she thinks, *I do owe my modeling career to him.*

"Buono. Here, let me tie it on for you." Turning her around, he stands behind her and ties the mask on her face. "Perfect."

"But I want to see what it looks like."

"My dear, you shall. At midnight. Please indulge an old man."

Though her face is covered, he can sense she is pouting. With a hand signal, he calls for the servers who placed a glass of wine in her hand. It appeases her. Yet he knows of her infidelities and betrayals, and so takes the precaution of having all of the mirrors in the palazzo removed, so he knows she can't cheat.

"If you will excuse me, I must see to other guests."

Though the guest is in his fifties, his youthful physique and glorious mane of shoulder-length hair reveals his identity. It is Rafael, a former business partner and cheat, who robbed his company's secret cosmetic formulas. That was ten years ago. He has assumed the identity of Capitan Scaramouche, a swashbuckling officer, dressed-to-kill in a black cape lined with red silk, a feathered hat, high boots, and sword in his belt.

How predictable. It will not be so easy to have him give up his mask. How fitting he chose such a disguise that so captures his true self: a cheat, a partner that betrays; a thief.

He strides up to his guest, tucking the crop he carries underneath his arm, while extending his soft leather glove in welcome. "Rafael. Good of you to come."

"Ah, yes! It has been a long time."

"Too long. Certainly too long to hold a grudge."

He nods.

"Please, join the party, but before you do, I beg one favor."

"Oh?"

"I have selected masks for some of my oldest acquaintances. I would be appreciative if you could see your way to exchange Scaramouche for another, which I have had made for you."

Rafael hesitates. "But I have had the entire costume designed around the mask."

"I appreciate that, and I assure you it will work with what I have made. Did you know that in Africa such masks confer power to the wearer? Besides, this mask contains gems which I assure you are real. You may keep these after the masquerade."

Through the slits that serve his eyes, the host assesses the greed of Rafael. He knows the authentic gems please him. With little thought, Rafael removes the mask and hands it to his former friend.

"Excellent! Come to my office and I will give you the new mask." As they walk, the host places an arm around his former rival. "There is one condition that goes with the mask." "What's that?" Rafael stops and turns to face Dottore.

He laughs to soothe the tension. "I merely ask that I put it on you without your seeing it and you do not attempt to look at it until midnight. Is that not acceptable to you?"

"Well, I suppose that would be alright."

"Wonderful! There are beautiful women, the best cuisine and plenty of wine for you to fully enjoy the evening."

They enter the lavishly appointed room. Thick red draperies cover the floor-length windows. Effusive light casts a warm glow on the opulent surroundings. Laughter, music, and fine wine create an ambiance that is conducive to conviviality. With a gentleness that belies his personality, Dottore Pesce maneuvers the mask onto Rafael's face and ties it.

All of the guests admire the beauty of their surroundings. After much research and inspection, he had chosen this 16th century palazzo because of its resemblance to his stays at Palazzo Borghese in Firenze. Exquisite Murano crystal chandeliers reflect off candles and the smooth polished marble floors.

As the midnight hour approaches, De Faruci stands on one of the balconies that lookout to the Rialto Bridge. He gazes up at the jeering moon and salutes it with the last remnants of wine left in his gold crystal goblet. The clock strikes the hour and he returns to the ballroom. It is time for the show to begin. He takes a deep breath, preparing for the entertainment that he had waited so long to witness. What makes the performance so very special after all these years was that his guests will also be privy to the denouement.

With the wave of his crop, he signals for all to unmask. There are squeals of delight, surprise, and laughter as dozens of guests reveal their true identities. He pays little attention, for it is not for them that he had hosted this fete. Instead, he seeks out Rafael and announces it was time for his unmasking. From the corner of his eye, Dottore spots Francesca, but he makes no move toward her. *One at a time,* he thinks. *According to plan. There is no need to rush. It is, in fact, preferable that she be forced to wait her turn. Anticipation can be brutal.*

From behind an elaborately carved screen, a server rolls out a full-length gilded mirror.

De Faruci guides his guest to the object. The sudden silence of the revelers alerts Rafael. He moves to the gigantic mirror. With the doctor's help, he undoes the mask and stares at his reflection. His quick intake of breath is audible in the crowded room. The thick mane of hair that had been his signature has been weeded out, and replaced with random plugs of coarse fuzz that stuck out in sparse patches over the top of his pate. His athletic face has crumpled into a sac of wrinkled and sagging flesh. His gaze is met in the looking glass from sunken eyes, hooded by droopy eyelids that barely do their job. His nose is broadened so that the overall impression is that he bore a striking resemblance to a pig; the symbol of greed.

He turns to look at his unmasked host and shudders. Signor's look is a poisoned dart that has made its mark. Rafael bolts through the room through the choked path of revelers and flees the palazzo, the swirl of a black cape and a wisp of its red satin lining a visual hemorrhage of the man who is absorbed into the blackness of this Venice night.

Signor rubs his gloved hands together. He enjoys the sensuality of the kit gloves as he moves them in a show of pleasure. This is the only sign that betrays his true feelings, for anyone searching his face is met with a tempered steel gaze.

He patiently awaits the reaction of this haughty beauty before him. She slowly crosses the room toward him. Her step is leaden. Having witnessed the man's denouement, she is quivering with fear. He feels a rush of resentment as she senses the truth of what is about to happen. Fear wraps around her like a shroud, making it hard to breathe. With trembling fingers, she lifts off the mask and is braced for the screams that follow. Instead, the unmasked strangers silently recoil with disgust. Panic tears through her. Amidst the sepulchral quiet that follows, with closed eyes, she raises her trembling fingers to her face to convince herself of the reality of her situation. She forces her eyes open, and the mirror confirms her fears. Her youth and beauty has been erased. Deep lines, like those on a piece of aged parchment, are etched on her once-smooth face. Jowls replace her firm neck and waddle onto her wrinkled décolletage. Wisps of her hair, trapped beneath the mask, have turned grey. Her face is branded with numerous brown age spots, from which spring stray long hairs. She crumbles to the floor, a heap of human refuse. The beauty has transformed into a haggard, ugly crone.

"Dottore knows best, eh?" Faruci laughs uncontrollably. The guests do not fail to detect the asperity in his tone. With the snap of his fingers, the servers are upon the young woman, lifting her to a nearby sofa. The musicians return to their music. Through the window of the palazzo, a nicotine-stained moon smiles. "Let us make merry!" Signor commands. The hired musicians pick up their violins, and the party wears on.

WEB OF DECEIT

"We boast our emancipation from many superstitions; but if we have broken any idols, it is through a transfer of idolatry."

Ralph Waldo Emerson

When Jared regained consciousness, he felt as though his body was encased in cement. It was his first hint of existence. For some unfathomable reason, his eyes were sealed shut. It was not like the crusted residue of deep sleep. Instead, the substance that weighed heavily upon his eyelids had the consistency of thick syrup or molasses. When efforts to blink away the gooey deposits failed, he thrashed his head from side to side, hoping to dislodge the sticky matter. Gradually, as he felt his muscles come alive, he shifted his position in the bed. With heavy arms he reached toward his face, using deadened fingers to scoop away the tacky mess.

He opened his eyes to blackness. He had no perception of his whereabouts. Time was a meaningless concept. There was only now. As the cobwebs of inertia lifted from his brain, he tried to pinpoint his location. Amidst the pitch-black space, memories revealed themselves in bursts of random colors, shooting out nightmarish pictures like the spinning designs inside of a kaleidoscope.

From the recesses of his foggy brain, he recalled his car tumbling over a cliff. He visualized rocks and hundreds of fir trees, and for a brief moment seemed one with the fleeing pine cones that spewed from the branches that had once been home. He relived the slow motion decline, wondering when it would end. Like a man drowning, his life experiences flashed before him, picking up speed as they progressed. He was watching his own life story that raced past him with astonishing clarity and speed, eventually hurtling toward darkness. And then nothing. The plug was pulled.

I can think, so I can't be dead. I'm in a coma in the hospital, he deduced. *That's why I can't see anything. It explains the weird sensations and the visions. How long have I been here? I have to wake up!*

Normally a man of action who made his own destiny, he felt trapped by his circumstance. Admittedly, he had been ruthless in his pursuit of business, and life in general. It was the only way he knew how to survive. He had been treacherous and made no apologies for it. Relationships and transactions had been made on the spot. Waiting was not an option. Considering his present circumstances, he tortured himself by asking *"How long can I stay like this?"*

Though robbed of his vision, his hearing seemed more acute

than usual. He recalled reading something about when one sense goes the others became keener. For now, the explanation satisfied him. And then he felt something cold brush his leg. His hand reached down to his thigh to insure himself that it was nothing more than a fly, or perhaps a muscle tick. Just as his mind was to swallow the logic, he felt it again. This time whatever it was lingered. He shivered, yet he resolved not to yield to the creeping panic rising in the pit of his stomach.

Some one pressed against me. That's a good thing. That means I'm not alone! In an instant, terror transformed into hope.

He waited for the touch. When whoever it was touched him again, he would reach out and grab him and not let go. That would prove he was still alive. It would demonstrate his efforts to pull himself out of this coma. For a man who was not acquainted with patience, the time crawled like a slug on a hot summer afternoon.

He lay in a state of exaggerated lethargy. He was unaware of the length of his fugue. His only companion was the steady pulsing of his heart. Eventually, he heard someone move. It wasn't quite the sound of a footfall; it was just a hushed noise. His ears reached out for proof. He convinced himself he was not hooked up to a breathing machine, and he was pleased that his condition must be stable. As his ears focused on the slightest of noises, they were welcomed by a very light padding across the floor. And then something hissed. It was a sibilant sound, like a tire losing air.

What hisses? A snake! Oh, God, not a snake!

As he forced rational thinking down his dry throat, he reminded himself that snakes didn't pad across the floor. They slid. This was not a sliding sound. As though to reaffirm his conclusions, the thing moved again, this time picking up its pace with a rhythm all its own. Step, step, shuffle, shuffle. With the lightest of steps, it drew nearer and then plopped down. *Was it resting? How far was it from him?*

His heart hammered in his chest. He felt numbness in his left arm. His fingers tingled. With each second that passed, a new symptom inflicted itself upon him. *Am I hav*ing a *heart attack?* He reached around the bed, seeking out the nurse's call button. It wasn't there. In the ensuing silence he concentrated on slowing his breathing down. *It's just panic,* he reassured himself.

Now that he had decided it was a thing, not a human that touched him, his direction shifted. Not about to subject himself to this thing's touch again, he focused on reanimating his legs.

He lifted the left one up to what he judged to be the ceiling. When this worked, he tried the right leg. Satisfied with the outcome, he drew them over the side of the bed and carefully stood. The sounds stopped. *Is this a game? Am I dealing with an intelligent creature?*

With outstretched hands before him, he began to walk. He inched across the icy cold floor, knowing that all rooms have a door. He would find the exit. If they saw he was walking, even if it seemed he was sleepwalking, they would attend to him. He would be rescued. It was a plan.

It hissed again. Then he felt something wet and slimy on his hospital gown. *It's spitting on me!* The sharp pain that ensued on his lower back where the spittle had landed frightened him. *What is this thing? If only I could see it! How can I fight something I can't see?*

He turned in another direction, still seeking a way out. After a few feet, his hands met with gossamer-like material that stuck to him. With effort, he withdrew the adhesive from his fingers. Trying to determine the measurements of the room, he reversed directions and went to what he hoped was another wall. Again he was received by a gauzy texture, totally unfamiliar to his senses. Throughout his explorations his enemy remained silent.

He calculated he was in a room no larger than six by nine. He judged his contact with the strange material to be the site of the outside walls. He was trapped in a space the size of a walk-in closet!

As he formulated this mental construct, he felt the now-familiar touch on his shoulder. Its light touch was like that of a butterfly flitting from petal to petal. Only butterflies glided through beautiful gardens amidst the shining yellow sunlight.

Frustrated, he sat down on the floor. As time hobbled by, he came to realize that he was neither hungry nor thirsty. That would be true in a coma, he rationalized. He felt his arms and hands for bandages that might indicate he had received an I.V. There were none. The typical plastic bracelet of an admitted patient was also nowhere to be found. He smoothed over his skin, seeking painful bruising or scarring. Again it was in vain.

All he knew was that he was alive and he was here in this abyss. He WAS. And he was not alone. His mind traversed the landscape of darkness and the unknown. He was terrified.

The sounds began again. Step, step, shuffle, shuffle. It was closing in on him.

Though he felt sure his pounding heart might not cooperate,

he decided to deliberately wait for contact. If the thing had meant to harm him, it would have already done so. He would calmly accept it. This time when he was touched, he reached back to his shoulder and felt its hairy essence. It was neither the smooth hair of a plush stuffed animal nor the cuddly soft hair of a puppy. His mind identified it with the harsh, bristle-like, scratchy, abrasive hair of a scrubbing brush used to remove the built up foods that stick to an outdoor grill. He shuddered. He grappled to hold on to his sanity as his heart accelerated. He was finding it harder to take a deep breath. Claustrophobia was taking over.

He conjured terrible images of what *it* could be. Images of hideous creatures swam before him. He envisioned whipping tails, razor-edged teeth, even the fangs of a mutated giant saber tooth. And amidst these horrific images he shivered from the bitter cold that crept into his bones. It was one more aspect of his newfound terror.

As the thing perched another leg atop his other shoulder he lost it. He tried calling out, "Nurse! Nurse!" but discovered he had no voice. Not a sound could he coax from his mouth. He tried repeatedly, but met with no success. Blind and with paralyzed vocal chords, he let the horror of his situation enfold him like a blanket.

It leaned in closer. He felt the icy cold breath of it inches away from the side of his cheek. As it exhaled, he cringed at the misty spray of its exhalation. It was repulsive. *What can I do? How can I help myself?* His questions were met with another up close and personal, *hiss*. A gurgling from deep within its throat made him gag. He knew what was coming, yet was still repulsed when it expelled its mucous secretion over his shoulder. The vile phlegm ran down the front of his gown. As the pain immobilized him, he opened his mouth and silently screamed in agony.

A visual image distracted his fear. Where it was once black and sticky, it now began to lighten. He was being allowed to see what was beyond his den of darkness. What he perceived to be a wall was not opening, but rather fragmenting as though it was a giant pixel in a photographic image. Particle by particle it vanished. As this transpired, he felt the thing release him and scuttle away.

His face met with a searing heat and blinding light from the fire that raged beyond. His breath came in rapid gulps as the extreme temperature shocked his cold body. Squinting through sensitive, smoke-filled eyes, he saw unimaginable things.

Wraiths of all shapes and sizes flew through the air, diving in and out of the flames. From fleshless skulls, red eyes leered at him. Grimacing eyes and bloody mouths contorted over skeletal bodies before him. The stifling air was swarming with screeches and howls. The amplified sounds emitting from these creatures were like none other he had ever heard.

Sensing the doorway would not remain opened, he stole the opportunity to survey as much of his prison as he could. The areas he had thought represented the corners of the walls were actually finely woven webs. Like the designs of fine lace workers, the webs were intricately fashioned in silky patterns that exceeded human handiwork. As the wall began to return to its former mass, a slithering movement from above attracted his attention there. Suspended above him was a grotesque black spider a good five feet in size, waiting to pounce and devour him. The three-dimensional window to what lay beyond magically incorporated into its former solid mass. He was trapped! *And I am not alone!*

His mind could not take in the horrors. It vacillated from slim hope to utter despair drenched in a terror so palpable that he felt weighted down. One moment he was unable to shake the idea that he was still in a coma. *Places like this don't exist,* he thought. He groped his way back to his bed and lay down. The panic he had tried so hard to avoid returned with a vengeance. His mind spun and his heart raced in his chest. His hands shook.

And then an idea so awful, so unthinkable, so alien to his thinking crashed in on him. *What if I'm hooked up to a machine? I could be here until my organs give out. I never signed a living will. I'm only fifty-two and I thought I had all the time in the world.*

"You've got that right," a thunderous voice responded to his inner thoughts. The booming voice reverberated in this canyon-like landscape. "You now have all the time in the world! You've got forever! Enjoy yourself. And welcome to your corner of Hell – a closet full of spiders!" The hideous laughing chilled his already cold body and pierced his fearful soul. Once again, he was hermetically sealed in blackness.

Jared was now soaked in his own urine. He began to shake and he gave in to the tremors that overtook his body. He tore at his hair in exasperation. He sputtered and choked on the words that could not be extricated from his mouth.

He jerked up in his bed, pulled his legs over the side and stood. The incredulity of his situation rushed over him like high tide at the beach. He knew it was coming and then upon him, but was powerless to avoid it. His conscious mind drew the logical conclusion: *This must be a nightmare! I will wake up!*

Not only was he trapped here, but he was locked in with a monster. Like a mounted butterfly in a glass case, he was pinned down and powerless to escape, and the devil himself could watch the scene whenever he chose.

When the light afforded him the opportunity to identify his enemy, it affirmed his fear. His enemy was upon him. His first clue was the thud that came crashing down from the ceiling. He heard another, *hiss.* From somewhere else in the closet he heard another shuffling. *Off to Buffalo,* he mentally sang. His conscious mind was holding on to its sanity by a fine thread. He was on the fringe of breaking, it was merely a silk thread which connected him to sanity and it was on the verge of snapping. Not a religious man, he nevertheless appealed to any savior who might listen. *Please don't let me be stuck in its web.*

Smaller hairy legs bristled against his bare feet. *Baby spiders*? He collapsed onto the floor and lay still. He was so very cold. He knew the spider was atop him now. Was the dampness covering his gown the ejection of its painful poison? Or far worse, was this glutinous slime now covering his stomach, its eggs? Would he be a breeding site, a nest for this spider's offspring?

He no longer shrank back in terror. A part of him struggled with the plea, *Don't touch me!* The synapses of his brain failed to work and his body was helpless to fight off the spider. His parched tongue was glued to the roof of his mouth. His prayers were no longer for freedom. He fervently hoped for a mindless, vegetative state; the end of consciousness and rational thinking. He ached to quell the incessant, surging terror that wracked his mind and body, but he could not force a shutdown of his mind completely. Incipient panic won out. As he realized and finally accepted this macabre scenario would play in reruns for eternity in this hellish prison, he wailed. It was upon him now, its hairy legs winding around his legs. His cry was a soulless, mournful sound that chilled the icy room. And no one heard at all.

RAGS, BONES ....

"Superstition belongs to the essence of mankind and takes refuge, when one thinks one has suppressed it completely, in the strangest nooks and crannies; once it is safely ensconced there, it suddenly reappears." – Johann Wolfgang Van Goethe

I hear the dinner bell ringing. They'll be bringing in my tray soon. I must hide this diary so no one will find it. I'm no longer foolish enough to think anyone will believe my story, not even mother. Poor mother, she doesn't know how to deal with this. Even after two years, it's beyond her. So as I write in this book, I will pray for her as I pray to understand why this has happened. I would like to know why God allows such evil in this world.

When it came to making soup, there was no contest. My mother, Jenny Kuta's vegetable soup took top honors. Her secret to the meatless meal? The best soup bones she could buy. Of course, being the mother of eight, she learned how to stretch her budget and make something delicious from whatever she could afford. And that meant she was a good customer of the ragman.

Mother told the other women in the neighborhood that the key to the soup's flavor was in the stock. Her soups boasted a rich broth that extricated every morsel of marrow from the bones. The carrots, turnips, onion, celery, and occasional potatoes were just window dressing. As the bones simmer in water, the liquid becomes intensely flavored. Three times a week mother would hover over her tall and narrow pot, stirring the broth for hours on end. The delicious results, which saved her money as well, were worth the effort.

Many like mother eked out a living by extending their food with soups and stews that took little to fill the empty bellies they had to feed. The potato became king. Many lived on boiled potatoes, fried potatoes, potato soup, or roasted spuds. In addition, these women literally gave the shirts off their backs to pay for the food, as used clothing was an item that was bartered with the ragman.

Secondhand clothes have a secret life of their own. Inanimate as they are, they retain the traits of those who wore them and quickly adapt to their new life. The ragman knew this to be true. For each rag, each vestige of worn fabric has its own identity, its own past, and its own unique future. Every cloth carries an unspoken connection.

Mother once told us about her grandmother's story of how immigrant Jews from Eastern Europe in 1900 collected, sorted, and sold secondhand clothing. As the Jewish peddlers made their way through North American city streets, they called out "Rags, Bones, Bottles!" One of the many towns visited was ours in Pennsylvania.

In this would-be city, the lanes behind the clapboard row houses were used by garbage collectors, those delivering coal, fruit and vegetable peddlers, the iceman, and the ragman. Several times a week, the families would gather to the alleys and offer their rags; twisted ropes of old pieces of clothing, now fashioned into long braids. The braids were never very colorful; no vivid reds or royal blues. That was impossible because the materials of which they were made had been worn, passed down, worn again, and beginning to fray to the point where the garment could no longer hold shape, and so was cut into strips and plied into plaits. Once collected, he would deposit the rags at a factory where they would again receive a new life as a quilt or other rug.

For all the contact the ragman had with the people, no one knew anything about him. "Rags, bones, zucchini, and tomatoes. Rags, bones, zucchini, and tomatoes," he hollered in a scruffy voice. We were all poor, so few of us questioned his unshaven and unkempt appearance. Even fewer took note of his strange eyes: one blue and one brown. He cut a dreary figure with his worn black pants and the rumpled brown shirt stuffed carelessly inside. He wore a frayed grey hat that was perched atop his head. It scared me to look him in those eyes.

Long before he reached the people, his mottled grayish horse would announce their presence with the clop, clop, clop of its hooves against the makeshift broken cobble-stoned streets. Though many of the children were now tenement dwellers, they vividly recalled vestiges of days on their farms, since foreclosed by the banks, when the horses plowed their fields. Seeing this steed, though seemingly blinded with large black eye patches, was a familiar and welcome sight. Sometimes the ragman would let the children pet the nag. I could tell that he was not a sincere person. I prayed on it and I received the feeling that something was just not right with the nameless ragman. One time I asked him his name and he said, "You don't need to know. I am the ragman. That will do."

I remember more than once telling Mother I had strange feelings about him. "He is really scary, Mother. I think he is evil. He doesn't even have a name or a family. We don't know where he comes from or where he lives."

I am sad to note she ignored my warnings. "Just take the strips, and when he gives you the money, buy us two soup bones; the biggest the money will buy. If there is change, buy whatever vegetable he has on sale," she said.

I have never been a trusting soul. Perhaps it was because I was nine when father walked out on us. Mother has been struggling to make a life for us since. It is not fair. Life is not fair. I do not trust men. When I am old enough I will enter a convent and dedicate my life to God.

God has been my savior in this place. He always has been. I remember two years ago when the event happened, that I was praying when the idea came to me. It was a revelation. I became aware that whenever the ragman came to town, shortly afterwards a child would go missing.

Of course no one would listen to me. The daily struggle of life and the turmoil that surrounded us prevented most people from thinking and coming to conclusions. When I tried to tell the neighbors, they went as far as asking me how I knew this to be true. I told them the truth: that "God spoke to me." They laughed and shook their heads. Even Mother told me, "Vicky, perhaps you *should* be a nun, since your head is always in the clouds!"

So I watched and waited. When spring arrived, the ragman made frequent visits to peddle his wares and make his trades. Minnie Satkowski was the first girl that was lost. Many thought she ran away to find a better life. She was fifteen and perhaps, they guessed, she had run off with a boy. Her parents, who cared for nine other children, assumed this was the case and no one ever tried to find her.

I noticed the mysterious ragman was partial to little girls. I watched when a girl would lean over to pay and he would meet her stance and inhale her scent. Up close I could see he was grizzled and graying. He smiled to the girls, but it was a smile that was wrong. *He is a dirty-minded man*, I thought.

I always obeyed mother. I knew that God wanted me to help her in any way I could. And so, on that special day, I reluctantly went down the stairs and out to the street where the ragman and his cart were parked. There were four other children there; three boys and another girl. From my vantage point, I could see the ragman leaning just a little too close over Olga, one of the neighborhood kids who was three years older than me and twice as pretty.

Slowly I made my way over to the wagon. The ragman raised his bushy right eyebrow as he noticed my approach. A sneer covered his face. I knew that I wasn't his favorite and that was just fine with me. I knew that the angels were protecting me.

"Ah, you are here for my bones, missy. Your mother, I've heard, makes the best soups from the bones you trade with your rags. Come closer and have a look." I didn't know if I shivered at his nearness to me, or because of the fact that his breath reeked of garlic and whiskey.

He continued, "The bones are large, and the marrow inside plentiful with flavor. It will make your mother's soup more wonderful than ever."

I didn't answer. I didn't like talking with him. Let him think I was a stupid kid not worth noticing. I nodded to him and held out the bundle of rags. The nameless ragman took the bundle and handed over the bones, which he wrapped in newspaper. I noticed the dark matter that crusted underneath his fingernails and I cringed. With the few coins remaining, I pointed to three turnips and the exchange was completed in silence.

I felt so angry that I had to deal with such a disgusting man. When I went back up to the kitchen, I tried again to tell Mother about the strange feelings I got about him. "Mama, he is not a good man. He looks funny at the girls. He is dirty and there is something about him... I think it is a bad omen that he is here..."

"Vicky, shame on you," Mother scolded. "He is poor like the rest of us, and we have no idea if he has a home or clothes. He is making a living the best he can, as we all do. You must not judge him by his appearance. God tells you that, you know. It is what is in your heart that counts, not the outside appearance. Do not be so judgmental."

"No one ever believes me," I cried. Swallowing my frustration, I moved on to finish my chores. It was more anger than duty that fueled my sweeping. I set out the heavy black cast iron pot to make the soup. As I was unwrapping the larger-than-usual bones from the newsprint, I wondered about their size. Where did the ragman get these bones? An idea came to me.

"Mama, can I go out for a little while?"

When Mrs. Wasnewski rapped on the door, I knew this was a signal for me to act. As mama set out a bowl of leftover soup for her friend, I slipped out. I wound my way around the streets of the town until I found the ragman's cart. I hid behind a building and waited. He began to move, slowly leading the horse down the cobblestones. I followed. I thanked God that the sun would be out longer in the sky now that it was summer.

After an hour, I watched him park behind the shed of a factory. He stood there, waiting, munching on a sweet tomato. I remembered the wonderful taste of the fruit that we would buy whenever it was in season. The juice dribbled down his chin and he smiled as though he knew something wonderful was going to happen. He had a secret; that was apparent. Before I knew it, Olga was standing by the cart again. The ragman was lifting her up onto the board where he drove.

"Where is she going? Is she out of her mind?"

The orange sun began to slip lower in the sky as the ragman's cart left the streets and made its way into the outskirts beyond the town. I followed carefully, so as not to be seen. Once the screens of houses were lost to me as cover, I trailed the wagon, crouching as I walked behind it. My back began to ache and my feet were sore in the thinned- soled shoes I was wearing. I grew weary as the wagon groaned on. I wasn't sure I would be able to stand up straight after stooping over for so long. At one point, I considered grabbing onto the back railing of the wagon, but I feared it would drag the progress of the cart and I would be discovered. All I could hear from the front was Olga giggling like a ninny. *What is she thinking?*

Looming ahead I could see an old, run-down, and seemingly abandoned house. As the cart neared it, the breeze carried a foul odor which worsened as we drew closer. The wagon stopped and the ragman lifted Olga down from the seat. They entered the shack and the ragman slammed the door behind them. As I crept toward the door, I heard a scream. It was as though a soul was being ripped from a body while the body was still alive.

I knew it was Olga. "God, please help me and tell me what to do," I prayed. The screaming continued and I covered my ears, waiting for a sign. It seemed to go on forever, and I was torn as to whether to burst into the shack or wait it out. My anxiety was eased when the screaming abruptly ended, and the door to the shed slowly opened and the ragman stepped outside.

"I know you've been following me, you little rat," he yelled. "There is nowhere for you to hide. You want to know my secret so bad? Come here, I will show you." Anger flared in his eyes.

I froze. Barbed wire coils of fear took my breath away. My mind told me to run, but my body would not obey. He came after me. I fell to the ground, pleading for my life. "Please, don't hurt me!" I wailed. I hated myself for being such a coward.

His silence was worse than if he had hit me. I didn't know how to react. My mind scrambled in all directions, thinking of the many ways I would be tortured. Instead, he offered me a hand up and held it as we walked to the shack. I knew that if I went inside I would never come out alive, so I began to pray for my sins. "Please let it be quick," I implored. "I don't want to suffer." He laughed.

The minute I crossed the threshold, my nose and stomach were delivered a punch. The air was foul with the vileness of desiccated flesh. I knew the secret of the shed and the ragman's life. There were benches and tables filled with body parts. Shin bones filled one table, while the arm bones of others occupied a place on an adjacent chair. I couldn't identify the others then, I had not the advantage of an education in anatomy. I smelled and saw the festering layers of rotting tissue. Veins and arteries were strewn about like unwound skeins of yarn. My shoes felt wet and I soon realized I was standing in the blood that saturated the dirt floor. I sensed a coppery sensation on my tongue. There was a cleaver on the table where a bone was being chopped. My eyes watered in the fetid air. I kept swallowing to avert gagging. It didn't help.

The ragman forced a disingenuous smile – a cruel smile of triumph - from which I recoiled in disgust. He burst out laughing, and then told me something I was totally unprepared for. He ordered me to remove my shoes. With trembling fingers I did as he demanded, though I shivered at the thought of what else he would make me do.

"You will be allowed to leave, but I advise you not to say anything about this." I was thankful he stayed on the opposite side of the room. He wore a look of cold shrewdness as he watched as I took in the horrific scene.

"These are hard times," he said. "I'm entitled to earn my living and to enjoy what I do. A little recreation, you might say. I offer no other explanation." He was gorged with self justification, which I could not understand. *This is the meaning of sin,* I thought. *Moral sewage. God help us and all those he has killed!*

With the knowledge I was not to be murdered I grew miraculously calmer, so I bravely asked, "Where is Olga?" He looked at the cleaver and the fresh blood that was spilled over the table. There was no need for words.

He continued, "No one will believe you, especially your mother." With a sweep of his hand he noted, "All this will be gone, so even if you tell there will be nothing to see." As an afterthought, he added, "Who would believe a child? Especially a homely one such as you."

That day changed my life. I am still visited by violent flashes of recall of the contents of that shed. I realize now that I am to be a martyr. This is what God requires of me until I can leave my material life and enter the convent. I spend my days praying and reading and educating myself the best that I can. I make lists of new words each day and memorize them, and test myself at the end of the week. It helps pass the time and take my mind off that horrible day.

I only wish I could have helped Olga, but I was powerless. Still, I accept the guilt and will continue to seek forgiveness from God.

I hear the clopping of the horse's hooves. A shiver runs down my back, bringing with it all of the memories of that terrible day. I look from my window, and sure enough I see him with his blinded horse peddling his wares. For just an instant I think he looks up to this third story window and I shrink back to avoid meeting those eyes. They are the eyes of a devil. Am I imagining it? I'm sure that he remembers me, and he probably laughs at me because they placed me here. He was right to think that nobody would believe a child.

Someday, someone will believe me. And if they don't, when I'm eighteen in two more months, they will have to release me and I will go to the convent and pray the rest of my life to erase what I have seen and what I know. I will beseech the Virgin Mary to help find a way to stop this fiend. I will plead with God to comfort those who have lost a child. I will say the rosary for them every day of my life. But I cannot pray for his rotten soul. I don't know that I ever will be able to. Will God forgive me for that?

I hear the trays being loaded onto the carts. Its dinner and I must hide this diary.

"Hungry, missy?" The nurse asks.

As she delivers the tray she carefully lifts the shiny domed lid that covers the dish of chicken. "Oh, I almost forgot," she adds as she lifts a cup towards me. "Here is something special your mother sent. Aren't you the lucky one? It's a bowl of homemade soup!"

There's no holding back. I'm retching as I hold my stomach in vain.

SCORPIO'S STING

"Superstition is to religion what astrology is to astronomy; the mad daughter of a wise mother." Voltaire

A sepulchral quiet reigned over the candlelit cemetery. The Catholic faithful, embalmed by their individual sorrows, moved slowly through the rows of graves. Their progress, impeded by the drenching rain, relied on bursts of lightning bolts that defined the autumn skies of Vienna and lit the paths between the broken headstones on their way to the repository of bones. The melancholy setting was an inherent part of their annual ritual, for it was November 2nd; All Souls Day, and they had come this year, as every year before, to offer their prayers for the souls of the dead.

It was a time not taken lightly, for they believed that only the tempestuous weather matched the churning of the souls waiting for eternal salvation. Relatives from near and far came to beseech God for these restless spirits to progress into the heavenly kingdom. This oversimplification of the Catholic Church's definition of "contrapasso" was what the masses understand.

Far away from the skeletal remains and tarnished souls of the charnel houses, a grand palace was filled with light as the inhabitants await a joyous event. If the mourners in the cemetery were coping with the aftermath of death, then the opposite was the case in this magnificent edifice. Yet, the two scenes shared the atmospheric electricity on that night. As lightening scissored the sky, the countryside loomed darkly. The chill winds of November made their presence known, buffeting tree branches against the windowpanes of the birthing room. Like claws scratching in anger, they added another element of gravity to what should have been a happy occasion. Nature had begun its hibernation early, and the wicked weather was cruel during its passage. Storm clouds battled the sliver of moon that hung tenuously in the threatening skies. The wind rose with an eerie whistling, and the downpour saturated the ground. If one judged by the temperament of the climate, it was not an auspicious time for a newborn to enter the world. The astrologers of the time confirmed this as they drew up the chart that noted the birth of the child on November 2nd, at 7:30 p.m.

The female child was to be a Scorpio - the sign associated with the constellation Scorpio, occupied by the sun from October 23rd to November 22nd. The eighth sign of the Zodiac is equated with intensity and power. Many hold that those born under this sign are said to have a complex, emotional, analytical, focused, determined, hypnotic and self-contained character. Yet it is also a character prone to extremity, jealousy, possessiveness, stubbornness and cruelty. Not only was the infant under the sign of Scorpio, but she was born on All Soul's Day. Since one's birth sign was believed to dictate the course of one's life, many foretold this child's ominous future. The timing of this Roman Catholic infant was of great concern. In accordance with the religious calendar, All Soul's Day held great significance. St. Odilo of Cluny established the festival c.998 to pray for those souls trapped in Purgatory (which was itself invented around this time to give ordinary medieval Christians some hope of avoiding Hell). Medieval Christians believed that most of even the faithful would go to Hell and that most of the saved would have to work out their sins in Purgatory before reaching Heaven. Therefore, a festival that encouraged prayer for their souls that might shorten their stay was as important as one that honored the saints. It appears that neither Boniface, Gregory nor Odilo was aware of the near juxtapositioning of these two new holidays with the ancient one of Samhain. The fact that amidst this metaphysical turmoil of contaminated old souls, a new soul would forage its way through such potential evil was acknowledged to be a contentious journey to say the least.

As the mother prepared for childbirth, the congregation in the cemetery proceeded to the charnel house, where the bones from the over–filled graveyard were stored. The doors were opened and they began pouring in, genuflecting amongst the bones while others knelt outside on the wet grass. In the dark, lit only by the candles burning on each grave, they sang the "Complaint of the Charnel-house," a hymn which appealed in a dirge-like manner for prayers. It was a heart-wrenching sound, which continued until nine o'clock when a messenger rang the bell for everyone to return home. Everyone knew that it is not wise to meet the souls which would be streaming home at midnight.

While the mourners wailed for the dead, Antonia had been born. This infant girl, the fifteenth and penultimate child of her parents, took her first breath on earth. The baby nurse swaddled the infant, checking every delicate feature. The bells tolled for the second time that night, as the cycles of life and death intertwined.

The cemetery was now vacant. The mourners had all gone home, but their work was not done. It was time for the ceremonies of the "veille." Each housewife spread a clean cloth on the dining table, where she placed hot pancakes, curds, and cider. The husband of the house made sure the fire was well banked up and placed chairs around it. Before anyone could go to bed, a band of singers known as the "chanters of the dead" went through the village, rapping at each door to enter and chant another hymn asking for prayers. A single candle in the window would guide the restless spirits on their journey from Purgatory. Should someone in the house wake in the night or hear murmur in the kitchen, he knew the ancestors were back, warming themselves at the fire or eating, for these lost souls were always cold and hungry.

Belief in this tradition was so strong it was depicted in grotesque drawings and etchings, revealing angry and confused spirits writhing in torment as they flew randomly across the roofs of houses and church steeples. Those who knew of the child's birth shuddered at the thought of an innocent soul struggling through this mélange of evil.

If the child's mother had grave concerns over the timing of her daughter's birth, she never gave lip service to such fears. Perhaps having fourteen children before the baby made her more complacent about predictions. The same could not be said of the baby's father, who was enslaved by the horoscope. The blessing of the child took place under the best of circumstances the very next day. Money was plentiful, and everyone who was anyone was present. Though some might have deemed the room filled with mirrors an ostentatious touch, it was doubtless elegant and represented the best that money could buy. Yet her father was absent, feverishly consulting with an astrologer over her chart. The godparents were also absent.

The years passed uneventfully, and the child was surrounded by her many brothers and sisters. As a child of privilege, she was accustomed to finery. Her mother's place in society was such that the culture of the time revolved around her desires. The young girl was acquainted with well-known writers and composers, though she showed no particular talent in either area. An ebullient soul, she played the harp to a degree, was versed in etiquette, and spoke Italian and French.

The feisty, straw-blond haired girl was eventually promised in marriage. She wasn't overly enthused. "But mother, he's not very attractive, is he?" she whined.

Gazing into her daughter's deep blue eyes, the mother says, "Ma petite, Antonia, it is a matter of politics. You will get used to him."

"Very well," she pouted.

"I know what will make you feel better; would you like to call in Mademoiselle Bertin? A new dress is just the perfect thing."

"Oh, yes. Let's send for her. When I marry him, will I still have her do my clothing? Can I still have my salon?"

"Why of course, dear. You will be expected to dress well and Mademoiselle Bertin is the best designer in all of Paris. There is no one who can design better than she."

Easily distracted with the promise of continued extravagance, the girl announced, "While I am waiting, I'm going to play with my dollhouse. You know mother, sometimes I think how very wonderful it would be to live inside of my dollhouse. It would be grand to just, I don't know, get away."

"Yes, dear," the mother absent-mindedly responded. Having fourteen other children to manage gave her little time to dwell too much on her blond beauty. She walked toward the opulent little mansion that had taken one year to construct. Each side of the three-and-one-half foot tall and five-and-one-half foot wide building was architecturally different, but the real coup was its exquisite furnishings. Real crystal, gold, and sterling silver accented the magnificent model. The house's walls across which was twenty-two carat gold leaf gilt, were filled with miniature oil paintings crafted by artists. The dining table, made from mahogany, was the host for silver cutlery replete with dinner and desert forks. Hand-painted porcelain Sevres plates and real goblets completed the service. It was fit for royalty, without a doubt.

Within the year the young girl married her intended. Though not of a serious nature, she felt chills each birthday that the country prepared for the contrapasso. Yet all fears were quickly extinguished each time Mademoiselle Bertin visited with new material for a new dress; and since the young girl never wore the same dress twice, the visits were frequent. Pearl-encrusted clothing replaced any temporary concerns with life outside of her grand home. Her husband's lavish presents, including a spectacular diamond necklace, confirmed her belief that all was right in her world. In fact, in many ways, she saw her life as an extension of the life in her dollhouse. She was insulated from the world amidst a life of luxury and pampering. Even when a scandal developed involving the diamond necklace, she dismissed it as not her concern. It was viewed as a misunderstanding and nothing more.

The years passed and her lifestyle changed little. Her wardrobe remained consistent, thanks to the dressmaker – until the day when the people filled the streets dressed in ragged torn clothes, screaming for food. She was astonished. *Where is this coming from?* she wondered. *How long has this been going on? Why hasn't anyone told me any of this?* When the new regime invaded her home and carted her off to prison, she was in a state of shock. She lost her name and was referred to only as either the widow Capet or Prisoner Number280. Her world was shattered. Her children were separated from her. She could not see her husband. Heavy bags draped her once-stunning blue eyes. Refusing to eat, she became emaciated, prematurely aged, and totally exhausted. Her richly embroidered gown was replaced by a stained and frayed black mourning dress. A mantle of gloom hovered over her cell. After all of the extravagances she had enjoyed in her life, it was despair had now come courting.

Then, just two weeks short of her thirty-eighth birthday, she was permitted to change into a brand new white chemise she had secretly saved. Though the dress was fresh, her person was not. She was aware of the smell on her body, her unkempt hair, and rough hands and nails. The humiliation was not enough for her captors. On the morning of $16^{th}$of October, a guard arrived to cut her hair and bind her hands behind her back. His eyes spit hatred. She struggled for composure as she was undressed and her shoulders were covered by a white fichu. Atop her prematurely-cropped white hair was placed a white pleated cap.

Out on the street, the air smelled corrupt. A sea of hostile faces taunted her on the Place de la Revolution. "Traitor," they screamed. The full reality of her situation slammed into her with a fury she had never experienced. Yet to those who watched her, she did not lose her presence that all came to know. With the dignity which her mother had instilled upon her, she ascended the scaffold. The thought flashed across her mind, *Could the astrologers have been right? Had I, at birth, been fated for this moment? Was this what father and the astrologers had known all along? Scorpio's sting was fatal!*

As she stepped toward the monster known as the guillotine, she inadvertently stepped on the executioner's foot. "Monsieur, I ask your pardon. I did not do it on purpose," she murmured.

The black hooded figure grunted assent. She placed her neck in the guillotine. She was ready when they called her name: Marie Antoinette!

WHAT A HOWL!

"Superstition is foolish, childish, primitive and irrational – but how much does it cost you to knock on wood?"

Judith Viorst, American author, newspaper journalist and psychoanalysis researcher

Primitive people have always relied on nature. It is how they have survived throughout the centuries. They work with the land and seem to thrive. And though modern technology has found its way, those still living in primeval settings maintain that interdependence. Much as they take the seed from the Tamarind tree, or harvest the mahogany for export, they extract the goodness from their environment and return the gift in many different ways. This is how it has been in Central American countries. It is the way it still is in Belize.

Everything about this cruise to the Western Caribbean was the same. Like the last time she was here, it was the spring. The weather was warm and beautiful. The cruise ship was afloat in the pristine waters that thousands flocked to for swimming, underwater photography, and scuba diving.

She had to admit that the brochures she and Bob had read describing the crystal-clear waters and white sand beaches along the 150-mile unbroken barrier reef in Central America sounded exotic and fun. On board, the gentle tropical breezes caressed her skin, and though it was warm, she shivered. Yes, the place was the same. Everything was the same –except Bob was missing.

Marcia swept a tear from her eye as these thoughts invaded her mind. Standing by the deck railing on the balcony of her cabin aboard the Royal Queen of the Seas, she experienced some of the initial shock when Bob had gone missing. It was followed by an overwhelming sense of guilt. She could not talk herself into feeling she had done all she could to find him. It was impossible to move forward in her life until she knew the truth.

Though the authorities had investigated and she had called in a private investigator, no one ever found him. So, two years later, here she was on the same ship heading back to Belize where her husband of twenty-five years had mysteriously vanished.

As the ship neared the harbor, Marcia made her way down the loading area, where the small tender would take passengers onto shore to await their respective tours or beach-going activities. Just like before. Only this time, she boarded the craft solo. Because Belize had no docks, the ship could not shore up on the land. It was not uncommon in the islands.

As promised, the air-conditioned bus was waiting in Belize City to take the forty passengers who opted for the tour to Tower City and the Mayan ruins at Lanai. She thought it serendipitous that the tour operator, who identified himself as Chino, was also the guide who had led her and Bob. When he took her hand to help her off the bus, she thought their eye contact registered familiarity. *Does he remember me and my husband?* She wondered.

Chino, who was working hand-in-hand with the cruise ship line, thoughtfully provided a cooler filled with iced bottled water. The line wanted to avoid dehydration from sun exposure at all costs.

The scenery had not altered. Evidence of poverty covered the landscape of the public highways. As they passed the fields dotted with impoverished housing and children playing amid the abandoned cars and roaming cattle, Marcia reflected for the hundredth time on her marriage to Bob. Everything seemed fine. The fiery passion that once consumed them both had calmed, but there was still a spark.

She tried to focus on what problems he could have been having with the construction business he owned. He had no major creditors chasing him for money; they did not go overboard in their spending either in his business or in their personal lives. She was sure that he had been faithful. He had talked about retiring someday to a place where he could roam the wilds and be totally free. She thought he meant someplace like Alaska, or perhaps a farm somewhere in the Midwest, but he told her on the cruise that the Caribbean was as good as any place and perhaps they should consider that. The children were educated and in their own businesses, and Bobby Jr. was now also – temporarily - heading his father's company. Until he returned. Everyone used that phrase. Until he returned.

The authorities in Belize were responsible for that little phrase. If there is neither body nor evidence of foul play, we must assume that he is still alive. *Perhaps,* they said, *he does not wish to be found.*

She played that thought over and over in her head. Does not wish to be found. The thought was abrasive. Yet even their pastor at home indicated that stranger things have happened in life. Was it possible? She guessed anything was possible. But was it likely? No. She definitely thought *no.*

As the bus pulled into the parking area, they were led to a small hut which contained their island crafts, jewelry, and assorted tourist items. They were ushered past these after the guide noted there would be time for purchases after their excursion. They walked single-file onto the ramp where two boats were docked. The open boats were covered with a canvas roof to offer shelter for those sitting on the bench-style seats.

Iced water bottle in hand, she boarded in the back of the boat. She scanned the crowd, noticing the tourists brandishing their digital cameras. The ride along the New River was quiet enough. She could have slept through this part of the tour. She was almost oblivious to the sites the guide was pointing out. She smiled briefly as they passed a colorful Toucan perched in a tree. She remembered the lecture about the mahogany trees, and was blithe about seeing the bulging eyes of a crocodile poking through the water between a score of lily pads. *This isn't what I'm here for.*

A huge bird Chino explained was a limkin screeched across the azure blue sky. The bird, said Chino, was a descendent of the prehistoric pterodactyl.

A half hour into the river ride, Marcia grew edgy. The captain of the ship deftly negotiated his way across the still waters. Soon they would come to the bend in the river where the boat would stop - just for her. Amid the lush vegetation, a Mennonite community had settled. Led by author Emory King, the group had established the site in the 1950s. As the boat docked she knew she had little time to waste. She had been cautioned by the government that the people here spoke any of seven languages, including German, Spanish, Spanish Creole, Garifina, or Carib with Yucatan dialects. Still, she had to try. Perhaps Bob had lost his way and found himself among these people. It was more logical than the alternative: that he would be living in the forest in the wild amongst all species of animals.

She could tell from the looks on the face of the tourists, they were not pleased to be kept waiting. She walked quickly into the village. An elderly man was waiting for her. She was excited when he greeted her in English. "Greetings."

"Hello," she said.

"I am so sorry to inform you that we have not seen anyone outside of our own people. The authorities have circulated a photo of your husband, but none of us have met him. We wish you the best in finding the answers you are seeking."

Marcia made a quick exit, once she realized there was nothing more to be said or gained by remaining here any longer. She returned to the craft, disappointed and sad.

The boat continued its way through winding passages on the river. After another twenty minutes, they disembarked the boat after reaching their destination, the village of Lamanai. The people were happy to greet the tourists, guiding them to their respective huts where they sold teak wood carvings, key chains, and tee-shirts that advertised *You Better Belize It*! As is often the case, their guide had to direct several of the tourists from early shopping, reminding them this activity was reserved for after their trek to the pyramids.

Picnic tables were already set up for the buffet lunch that would follow. The museum of Yucatan artifacts, filled with pottery, was still closed, waiting for the walking portion of the tour to end. Marcia was glad for that. She did not want to waste time looking at the figurines and pottery of the Mayan site, no matter how interesting it might be. Not while she was still looking for her husband.

And so they began. The entire jungle was painted in beautiful shades of every green imaginable. Huge fronds of saw palmetto, palms, and banana leaves brushed against her arms as she forded the jungle, headed for the Yucatan temple and ruins dubbed "the castle." Drooping vines frequently got tangled in their hats, while gnarled tree roots spread over the floor of the ancient civilization slowed their progress. Others on the tour joked about having the fortitude to climb up to the top of the structure, where they could get a glimpse of Nicaragua. The pyramid-like building still stands from the second century B.C. Chino said that some call it the "Empire State Building" of its time.

But she was not there to duplicate the climb she had made years ago. Instead, she waited for the bend in the beaten path that would take her to them. The dirt trail was uneven. She carefully trod the occasional stones that divided the footpath in two. The heavily worn walkway wound in circles, and at times she had found herself ascending little inclines, only to be followed by descending drops into a gulch. She had to watch where she was walking to avoid injury.

Periodically, Captain Chino shared his botanical knowledge by pointing out a plant or tree that was effectively used for medicinal purposes. He noted the papaya fruit trees and cashew trees. Cutting open a papaya, he explained that the meat was surrounded by a liquid which they were told burns to the touch. "The jungle, much like life, has both good and bad elements," he said. He added that the meat of the fruit is exported and used to make jams.

As she passed the unique strangler tree, she felt it was a symbol of the hold this place had for her family. "It is the function of this tree to choke other surrounding trees," Chino explained. "Its seed is deposited on the host tree by a bird or insect and it grows a tiny root that twists down the trunk. It is a very unique species." *Belize may be a paradise to some, but for me it is a nightmare.*

As their hike progressed, she felt the feathered foliage of the tamarind tree graze her shoulder. Its tiny red and yellow flowers and brown fuzzy pea pod added a dash of color in this sea of green. The tamarind tree produces edible, pod-like fruit, which are used extensively in cuisines around the world. Other uses include traditional medicines and metal polishes, while its wood can be used in carpentry. Beside the paste from the tamarind, Chino laughed as he told of the rather potent drink "tamarindo," which could be made from the tree.

As they paused on one of these mini information sessions to sip from their iced water, she heard it. They all heard it: a uniquely shrill scream. It was repeated three times, as though it were some kind of alarm to others in its tribe.

In spite of the ninety-eight-degree weather this sunny May afternoon, Marcia felt a sudden chill. In silence, Chino beckoned them to follow him up the side of a small cliff. Marcia recognized the howler monkeys. They were near, and soon Captain Chino would lead them to one of the hills they populated. It was déjà vu.

By the looks on their faces, many of the tourists were intimidated by the shrieking, rasping sounds of the monkeys. Yet she knew with certainty that many would forego that fear, that intuition of something wild and primitive, and climb to get an up-close-and-personal look and photograph this unusual breed. She was reminded of the phrase "the forest primeval."

She knew this because that's what Bob had done. It wasn't enough for him to climb part way up like the others did. He went all the way up. When some came running down the hill almost as fast as they had ascended, those who remained at the foot of the hill laughed and teased them. Slowly, one at a time, the more daring who had remained returned with memorable pictures. But Robert never came down. When Chino climbed to the area where Robert had been, he searched with no sight of him.

Later, the authorities duplicated Chino's efforts with the same disappointing results. Now she didn't know if she had the courage to go the way he did; she did not want to be lost forever, though she greatly missed Bob. All she wanted was an answer. To have some kind of understanding.

"Look up there," shouted one of the tourists. "That really big one. He looks different than the others."

As he spoke, the monkey in question jumped into another tree in hiding. Captain Chino said he had never seen one so large, but speculated that he was probably the leader of the tribe. Perched in niches of the cave, the monkeys lived in herds of ten, led by a dominant male. The crowd noted the protruding jawbone, which Chino explained holds the unique voice box that is responsible for their intimidating sounds.

"Let's get closer," one young man shouted. A group of others followed, cameras focused on the quest for the especially large howler monkey.

Now is the time, she thought, but she could bring herself no farther than half way up the hill. Still she noted the largest monkey, the leader, sat still, watching her from his perch high above. She feared that he might swoop down upon her, and so she stopped and slid slowly down the hill. Just as she had feared, he jumped to a lower branch. Her heart jumped. She could see him clearly now, and he was decidedly much taller than the others. She noticed the nails with which he clung to the branch were long and jagged, more human in nature than animal, she thought. She could not see his toenails, or she would have had the same reaction. Because he was intertwined in the leaves of the trees, she could not discern a tail.

At Captain Chino's command, the group was led down the hill and back onto the path that would take them to the temple. She trailed behind. Once the group began their ascent of the temple, pausing to take photos along the route, she scurried back to the hill of the howler monkeys. He was waiting. He sat midway, peering out from an apparent hollow or shallow cave. He knew she would return. From the recesses of his brain, he felt some connection to this human.

He screeched that terrible howl three consecutive times. It terrified her, but she continued walking up the embankment. She had to find out what mystery was here. She had come all this way for an answer, and she had to preserve her sanity and move on. And then, as though the animal had read her mind, he jumped out of his hiding place. She noticed pink flesh beneath some of the hair. He tilted his head and looked at her in a quizzical manner. He was trying to make an instinctual connection.

She was now only twenty feet away. He had been hiding his head in his hands. She began to tremble.

"Hello? Robert?" she said feebly. "Please, Robert, is it

you?" Her legs trembled. She didn't know how long she could stand at this angle.

Again, the creature tilted his head as if trying to remember her face.

She swallowed hard and tried again with more confidence. Using a stronger more urgent tone she demanded, "Robert, is that you?"

The monkey removed his hairy paws from his face and looked down at the figure before him. He stared into her eyes and she nearly fainted. The abnormally large howler monkey had beautiful blue eyes. Was she imagining it, or was the hair that covered his head intertwined with that which covered his chest and face, revealing a more human look? The abnormally long and downwardly curled fingernails seemed out of place with his brethren. His hairy lips were small and tightly closed. But just as she began to doubt any human characteristics, he jutted his face forward and broke into a wide grin, exposing perfectly formed teeth, save for the gap between his front incisors.

She recalled the dental work Robert had done before their last trip, and the fact that the dentist wanted to close the gap, but her husband had refused. "I don't want some fake appliance," Robert explained. "Leave the gap, and work around it."

Could this be a coincidence of nature? Could a monkey have the same physiognomy? How likely was that? Body hair and posture was one thing, she thought, but dental work?

Before she could ponder this thought any further, the creature stood erect and screeched. All the while he smiled at her. She detected other howlers in the nearby hills who responded to his howls. He seemed alert to his role as leader. He jumped to a nearby tree and gracefully swung his way across the jungle. Two others followed.

Chino had been standing behind a nearby palm frond. He ran up to her. She pointed and he smiled knowingly. "I've been watching. Madam, when you live in nature, as we do here, bad things don't happen. Not to worry. Perhaps this creature is truly home. I think you may have found what you were seeking. Nature takes care of us. How do you think man has survived for so long?"

NAILED!

"Superstitions are habits rather than beliefs."
Marlene Dietrich (German born American actress, 1901-1992)

When ten-year-old Piper and her maternal grandmother showed up on the front porch of Cousin Geraldine's home, they were confused to find a funerary wreath hanging on the door. Neither knew what to expect. They were admitted into a living room filled with people wearing black. The focal point of the subdued room was a small mahogany casket in which rested the corpse of a delicate-looking baby boy, dressed in a light blue outfit. Two nuns with bloated faces stared out of their starched white dimples, which framed their stark black floor-length habits. With each movement, their rosary beads swayed in accompaniment. They somberly acted as unofficial guardians of the dead infant. This image would be indelibly etched on the mind of young Piper.

Over the years, she had visited Geraldine many times, observing how she coped with the tragedy. An untrained, yet self-proclaimed artist, Geraldine sought refuge in a small bedroom of her Cape Cod house, which she transformed into her artist's studio. The hefty blond woman did not draw portraits, nor did she sculpt. Water colors were not her forte either. She did not sketch in charcoal, nor did her palette consist of enamels. Instead, she had devised a new form of art: nail paintings.

It wasn't long after Geraldine began her craft that she again became pregnant and delivered another healthy baby boy. A daughter soon followed. Year after year, Piper watched her cousin's art collection grow. Few visitors had ever seen the artwork; only family members had been privileged to see the in-house exhibit.

Though Piper had no formal art training, she was fascinated with her cousin's unique and colorful collection. And as her relationship with Clay had developed, she thought more and more about trying on this kind of art for size. She researched all the superstitions about the use of fingernails, referred to as onychomancy. She learned that the form of divination deals with fingernails and clippings, which are used for magical workings. She read that love spells could be cast by laying salt on the ground and sprinkling fingernail clippings upon it during certain cycles of the moon.

Once Piper was committed to an idea, she researched and collected as much information as possible. Her advanced reading revealed to her that the use of fingernail clippings would ensure that the spell affected the right person. The books said that greedy people had crooked fingernails, and the shape of the half-moon on the fingernail at the base is an indicator of longevity. It fascinated her that the women who knew the mad monk Rasputin, who influenced the latter days of the Russian Emperor Nicolas II and his wife Alexandra, would gather his fingernail clippings and sew them into the hems of their dresses for good luck. Without a doubt, the belief that fingernails held a supernatural power was practiced long before her cousin's curious dabbling.

Piper's new art form required little in the way of supplies. It was especially simple since, as a manicurist, she already dealt in the medium. The clippings were free. And when Clay wasn't able to see her, the project would consume the lonely hours waiting for him to call. She never actually intended to use them in any nefarious way.

"Piper, your client called and has to cancel. And Bobbi can't make it in. Her son has a high fever. Could you take her appointment?"

"Huh? Sure."

One look at the woman who was walking to her table threw her for a loop. *Is this where fate stepped in?* she wondered. She recognized the svelte-looking blond with high end clothes and expensive jewelry to match. The emerald brooch on her suit lapel must have been six inches long, with a thick pin attached. Money oozed from her pores. Piper's nocturnal visits to Clay's office had familiarized her with the family photos on his desk. The blond sitting in her chair was his wife! A brittle edge of resentment washed over Piper.

She reacted quickly. "Let me take your jacket," she offered. "I'll be right back," she said as she went to the closet in the rear of the salon. As the woman began talking about an upcoming European trip, Piper raged inside. *You witch,* she thought. *That should be me going. He doesn't love you.*

She immediately pulled out her nail clippers. As she suspected, the red shiny fingernails were quite long. *Perfect for cutting.* All she had to do was convince the wife that one or two were weak and ready to break and so they all should be trimmed to a uniform length and she could collect them for a possible future project. *Just in case,* she thought. *I need to cover all my bases in the event Clay continues his resistance.* Not that she really wanted to move forward, but the way things in her personal life were going, she had to have a resolution. She always hated waiting.

Piper carefully clipped the nails at an even length. Then, as she dipped the woman's hand into the nail softening solution, she expertly collected the clippings, slipping them into a plastic zip-lock bag. The other girls at the salon had laughed at her when she first started the practice but she didn't care. As the wife sat waiting for her newly polished nails to dry, Piper slipped into the office where she located the woman's cell phone number, jotted it onto a notepad and shoved it into her pocket.

Clay called that evening.

"When am I going to see you again, Clay?"

"It's not that simple. I do have a wife you know."

"Oh, I know. And so did *you* when you began this."

"It was a mutual interest, my dear. Don't blame it all on me."

"Fine, there was chemistry between BOTH of us. So, when can I see you?"

"Maybe next week, I'll call you."

"Maybe? And that's it? "

"What else did you expect? You knew how things would be; when there is time we can be in each other's company. Otherwise, I have a life and a wife."

It was a low blow. Piper swallowed hard and said goodbye. She had no choice. *Obviously he's been stringing me along and he is never getting a divorce. Perhaps it's time for an art lesson.*

She went into her bedroom which was filled with colorful artwork. In the style of her cousin Geraldine, there were pictures of butterflies, hands, flowers all shaped and filled in with painted human fingernails. While most of the nails were hers, she often relied on her customers to fill in the pictures. None of the works were enhanced with magic. Tonight, though, she would need the nails she had collected for other darker purposes. She felt a momentary prickle of disquiet about her intentions which was quickly replaced by a cold splinter of guilt. It passed rapidly.

She had read numerous books about the topic of onychomancy. And although she never thought she would pursue such drastic tactics, the anger surging within her prompted her in that direction. She took her time sketching the figure of a tall man with black clouds sagging down from the dismal sky.

At work the next day, she managed to convince Janelle that her navy blue nails needed a manicure and she offered her services. Janelle accepted, and now Piper had the makings of another color for the design. Since she had been doing this art – minus the magic - for a long time, she was able to draw from her large stash of colored nail clippings. She found black, cobalt blue, white, and platinum. *Everything has to be just right.*

The weekend was only a day away, and Piper listened to the weather report. Saturday was to be a perfect day for outdoor activities. That meant that he and his wife would take out their sailboat on the bay. Using the prepaid disposable cell phone she had purchased, she called the wife's cell. It immediately went into voice mail.

"Mrs. Haskell, you might be interested to know that your husband is seeing other women. I don't mean one woman, but several. I strongly suggest you meet me at 7:00 a.m. on Monday at Royal Café on Martine Ave. I'm helping you out here; you have a chance to get ahead of him before he finds out you know." She paused. "Just in case you decide to file for a divorce." Piper drove past the mall, stopped the car, and tossed the phone into the trash.

After work on Friday, Piper drove down to the marina where the *Carol Lee* was moored. She had changed clothes at work, trading her black pants and top for black sweats and a matching hoodie. Glancing around her, she saw no one at the dock. She climbed on board. Everything was ready for a sail. She had to be certain Clay would take his wife out tomorrow to allow her to plan every last detail and visit his office. She knew the couple spent weekends on the boat, so her timing was not threatened by a surprise visit. Once they set sail, Clay would not return to the office until very early Monday morning, and she would be waiting. She barely slept Sunday night.

At 5 a.m. on Monday, Piper let herself into the office. This was facilitated by the fact that Clay had given her a key to the office where on certain nights they would meet. She had surreptitiously made a second copy in the event he asked for the original one back. She took with her some food and drinks and was careful not to remove her gloves for any reason. Instead of using the bathroom outside the waiting room, she went out behind the bushes and cleaned up using plastic bags.

By 6:45, she heard the office door open. By the footsteps she could tell it was Clay. She waited behind the door for him to enter the treatment room. "Hi, there, Clay."

"My God, Piper. What are you doing here? Are you crazy? My wife could have come in..."

"I don't think so. She wouldn't lower herself to work here, or to even visit you here. She's first class, you know. Upper register and all."

Piper detected the fear in his eyes. A reservoir of rancor burst and she lost control.

"Look, I promise I will call, honey. We'll see each other soon."

As she swung around to face him, she thrust the sharp end of the brooch into his neck. A thin geyser of blood erupted, spilling down his shirt and trickling onto her gloves. She felt electrified.

"I don't think so, Clay. I'm tired of waiting."

He grasped his throat with both hands, trying in vain to stop the profuse bleeding. Piper pushed his hands away and kicked him in the shins, sending him to the floor. A strangulated, high-pitched squeal erupted from his throat. She thought he was calling for the police.

Piper watched and waited for him to die. It would be at least another hour until the receptionist would find him. From her pocket, she extracted a plastic bag from which she scattered a few of the *Fire Engine Red* nail clippings she had collected from his wife's manicure. Acting upon a craven impulse, she stabbed him with the pin again, this time twisting it to ensure he was dead. She did not remove the weapon. She knelt down and felt for a pulse. There was none.

Then, in the drawer she deposited three lace thongs she had randomly stolen from lockers at her gym. Rays of sunlight shimmered through the office windows as Piper locked the door behind her. Glancing at her watch, she saw that it was 7:30 a.m. The wife should be on her way to the Royal Café – if things went right. It didn't really matter if she showed, just as long as she was not home and had no alibi for the time of the killing.

Back home, Piper finished gluing the last red nails over the figure of the body in her picture. She breathed a deep sigh of relief. Her mother had often expressed the notion that life was one big waiting line. "A woman waits to finish school, then she waits to find a boyfriend, and then marriage. Then she waits for a child and then for that child to grow up. The waiting is horrendous."

Piper agreed. If she hated anything it was waiting. By standing by in anticipation of the world and others to make decisions she was in constant high anxiety. It was vital to take control. She congratulated herself on doing just that with Clay. *No more waiting, you jerk. You had your chance and you blew it. Players like you never win.*

Her thoughts were interrupted by a news break on the television: "This just in. Noted dentist Clay Haskell was found dead in his office this morning. He seems to have been murdered with a very large and pointed stick pin. CSI investigators are now processing DNA found at the crime scene and questioning his wife as to her whereabouts at the estimated time of the crime. As more details emerge, you can learn more about it on our 11 p.m. newscast."

FOR THE LOVE OF JERUSHA

(From a member of the Secret Drawer Society)

"The root of all superstition is that men observe when a thing hits, but not when it misses."

Francis Bacon, Sr.

It seems that all I ever do is wait. Time has no meaning any longer. I don't mark it by the changing seasons. I have lost count of the once-flaming red and yellow leaves floating to the ground and dying there. The sounds of the acorns tumbling from the trees, falling and bouncing off the roof no longer teases my imagination as I hear the brown and grey squirrels scurrying across the ground to store their treats. The innumerable pure white snowflakes that drape the inn and surrounding pathways fail to ignite any passion, or regret of what I have lost. Nor do I calculate the minutes and days and years by the hands on the clock, but rather record the passage of time by the never-ending parade of people who march in and out of these rooms. I marvel at their wardrobes, noting the changes in dress lengths and breeches. The coifs they don are so very strange to me. Even their speech strays far from the King's English my contemporaries utilized in my lifetime. These differences, in some cases what I would term aberrations of social behavior, are the only means at my disposal to discern time.

Although I realize it has been a long time and that I know he's not coming back, I ache for his face, his arms, his love now just as I did back then. My love, why did you not return?

I remember the day he left, looking so handsome in his uniform. His sincerity touched my heart. Surely the British Isles cannot be such a lifetime away? How can a heart such as mine exist in such torture? How much can I be expected to bear?

I know the answer. My waiting has come to an end. I must find someone else. I must push the boundaries of my confinement beyond this room and house and reach out to another who is equally lonely and needful.

Someone is coming. I must observe.

"This is the room you requested, sir. Number 9."

Accepting the key the man nods and seeks confirmation. "Jerusha's room?"

As he lays the suitcase onto a stand, the younger man concurs, "Yes, Mr. Nichols, this is where Jerusha, called by some the Belle of Sudbury, lived." After a meaningful pause he adds, "And where many guests claim she still walks."

"I hope so," Nichols mumbles.

"You do know about the secret drawer, sir?" Not waiting for a reply, he explains. "Some guests who have seen the spirit of Jerusha have reported her haunting. Since the 1900s, visitors have crammed little notes of their experiences written on bits of paper into every nook and cranny of this old inn. One ghost hunter found almost one hundred descriptive accounts of encounters hidden in room 9 alone."

I have never believed in ghosts until I read about Longfellow's Wayside Inn. A mere thirty minutes from Boston, I came here hoping I could free myself from the thoughts of my imminent divorce from Adrianne.

I know I am not the first to seek comfort and refuge here. The poet, Henry Wadsworth Longfellow, who came for a rest to recover from his wife's death and to find inspiration to

overcome his writer's block, was a guest in 1862. This was the source of his book, Tales of a Wayside Inn, 1863 which he wrote in the hotel's parlor. In fact, with its then creaking floors and weather –stained walls, it's been said he described it as an "old Hobgoblin Hall."

Nichols removes his clothing from the suitcase and stows them into the drawers and closet in the room. It is lunch time, and he is famished. He heads down to the dining room for lunch. The menu offers traditional food, so he orders the inn's lobster pie with sherry and crumb topping. He washes it down with the Wayside Inn's draft beer. The waiter invites him to check out the history of the inn in the lounge area of the check in desk.

The well-worn pages of the inn's recorded history indicate the horde of visitors over the years. The second page details the identity of Jerusha Howe. As part of the inn's four generations, she was the sister of one of the owners and was an accomplished pianist. Those who knew her spoke of her as the "Belle of Sudbury."

Legend has it that she fell in love with a British soldier, who vowed after returning from the British Isles he would marry her. She never gave up hope, pined away for him, and never married anyone else as she waited patiently for him to return. While she continued to live her life, enjoying her musical abilities, tending to her duties, her love life was frozen in time. After spending forty-four years of living and working in the house, she died a single lady, whose spirit still searches for love.

After strolling the property and enjoying a fine dinner, he heads to Room 9. There he is confronted with the scent of oranges or some type of citrusy fruit. *Her perfume,* he guesses.

Strange, he thinks, *since this is autumn and this New*

England autumn is rife with apples. But I know the scent of an orange, and an orange it is.

Striding over to the desk, he extracts his notebook and begins writing. "My first night."

His thoughts are interrupted by the tinkling sounds of piano keys. It is a short little ditty, nothing elaborate or indicative of a concert pianist, but rather a rudimentary tune with a melody of long ago. He recalls seeing the piano downstairs and attributes the distance to the faraway sound of the music. He is lonely. He wonders, *Does loneliness make for a more conducive or receptive state from which one can make contact with a ghost? If only I could see her beautiful face. I'm sure the picture in the book does not do her justice.*

The next morning, he casually mentions the music to the innkeeper who smiles. "I'm sure you did experience it, sir. It's not uncommon. Many in the Secret Drawer Society have indicated as much. My advice is to sit back and relax. It is not often one can find a place of peace and contentment. And Jerusha is a gentle soul."

The next morning, he makes another entry in the journal. "Only the citrus scent and the music were experienced last night."

Following a rudimentary breakfast he returns to the large red volume of the inn's history.

As he flips pages he recalls his own abandonment by his ex-wife. *Back in Jerusha's time, love was forever. Not anymore. Life and love are far more complicated today. Nothing seems to last. It is the disposable society. Only a soul that has known the betrayal, the deep aching of the heart could come close to understanding Jerusha.*

The afternoon passes quietly, filled with long walks and reading. Though the window is closed to the brisk autumn air, a current of air brushes over his resting face. It is quickly followed by the now-familiar scent of oranges. *I will not open my eyes,* he resolves.

That was all that came of the night. He is happy, but he is anxious for more; much more. The weekend is over and he dreads leaving the next morning, but a plan begins to form. He begs the innkeeper for the same room for the next two weekends and is greatly relieved his request is accommodated.

The days at work are endless for him. He clocks time by the remaining hours until he can return to the Wayside. His patience wears thin, until the moment he is driving the distance from Boston back to Sudbury for he now seeks more personal contact. He talks to himself as he drives. *I feel sure that Jerusha senses my presence and will soon make contact. I hope that she likes me. Perhaps, we can become close.*

Tonight I am ready and hopeful. My mind is alive and I can't shut down my thoughts.

I force myself to close my eyes and sure enough I am eventually rewarded with the citrusy scent. I am lulled into sleep when suddenly I am acutely aware of a presence in the bed. Something has slipped under the sheets and is touching me. A leg? It is cold. Very cold, but it doesn't matter. It is almost seductive and very romantic. I think she does care for me. If only I never had to leave you again, my sweet Jerusha. I would take care of you forever. If only there was a way that I could be sure we would find each other. I'm not afraid, my dear. No. Not at all.

My love, I cannot lose you either. The human heart is immutable. I know that you will forgive me. We will have all eternity to be together. There is no other way. Neither of us will ever be lonely again.

He feels the quilt move aside. She has risen from her place beside him. He does not see her translucent figure hovering above him but he senses her presence. He understands what she must do, and he accepts it. He welcomes it, for nothing else matters. He finds no reward in his profession or his personal life. She has become his world.

He prays that she is quick as she plies the pillow onto his face. He doesn't struggle. He welcomes the act, and so his struggle becomes one of appreciation. He knows what is happening is out of love. He breathes deeply into the pillow, hoping for the ending, and then the beginning.

The morning sun winks into Room 9 and the maid is knocking at the door. It is 10 a.m. and she needs to clean the room. There is no answer. She tries again, knocking harder and alerting the manager.

"Marie, what are you doing?" Stop making so much noise. What's wrong?"

"Sorry sir, but the gentleman is not answering."

"Use your pass key. Here, let me do it."

"You think the guy skipped without paying?"

"No, he always pays up front. I just want to be sure he's okay. Mr. Nichols did not leave without saying goodbye or making another reservation for the next weekend. That is not like him. He always books ahead."

The manager holds his hand motioning for Marie to stand back. "From the look of things, he has permanently made Room 9 his home."

As the maid follows the manager into the room, she gasps.

A pillow was covering the body of a man who was not moving. But what was more shocking was that beside him in the bed was the definite imprint of another body, smaller in size, and one long black strand of hair lay on the adjoining pillow. Mr. Nichols' hair is blond.

Had Jerusha finally claimed her lost love?

THE HEADLESS WOMAN OF ST. ANGEL'S BRIDGE

"Superstition, bigotry and prejudice, ghosts though they are, cling tenaciously to life; they are shades armed with tooth and claw. They must be grappled with unceasingly, for it is a fateful part of human destiny that it is condemned to wage perpetual war against ghosts. A shade is not easily taken by the throat and destroyed." Victor Hugo

Romantic literature has always encompassed the delicate issue of love. Whether the unrequited love of Tristan and Isolde, love lost, as Poe's Lenore, or the passionate affairs of Casanova, we are tantalized by the fragility and lure of this elusive emotion. This is particularly the case for the foreign traveler, for there is something that attracts the lonely heart to the legends of the untimely death of a young, vibrant, and beautiful woman in a land that is far from home.

Such was the case with Justin. Though he had come to Rome to study medicine, he quickly found himself drawn into the history and culture of the land. The ancientness of the city, the flavors of the country, and the climate of the Mediterranean oozed up through the cobblestoned streets and soaked the bricks and mortar that built edifices like the Forum and the Coliseum. His mind was afire with the events of the past. Rome was a city that saturated the senses.

He had been studying with a fervency that worried his instructors. "Take some time off," they advised. "Explore the city. Eat! Drink! Fall in love!" Had it not been for the severe headaches he had been suffering, he might have ignored the well-meant advice. But when neither pills, nor extra sleep, nor miles of walking seemed to alleviate the stress, he decided to follow their suggestions.

And what a great idea it had been! He walked to the Coliseum and imagined the roar of the crowds, the bloody gladiators, and the ferocious lions. He followed the worn tracks of the horse-drawn chariots at the site of where the Circus Maximus was held and easily envisioned the cheers of the people rooting for their favorite in the heat of a summer's day.

It was midterm of the semester, his break had just started, and he had found himself wandering the streets of the Centro Storico in the area of the Piazza Navonna. Starved as he was from human contact and life, he was consumed with the colors, the sounds, and the jovial laughter that surrounded him. This was the magnetic heart of the 2,000 year old city which stood above an ancient stadium. Here he sat by the Pantheon, gazing at the tightly-knit web of streets on the right bank of the Tiber River. Teeming with small shops, markets, restaurants, and tourists, the area with its fountain was the subject of countless photographs and wishers who dropped coins into the bubbling waters.

The temple is fronted by a massive pedimented portico screening which appears to be a cylinder fused to a shallow dome. Only from the inside can the true scale and beauty of this building be appreciated. In the 7th century, Christians claimed to be plagued by demons as they passed by, and permission was given to make the Pantheon a church. Justin could relate; he too had been haunted by the demons that manifested in the infernal headaches. That day, the edifice was lined with tombs ranging from a monument to Raphael to huge marble sarcophagi holding the bodies of Italian monarchs.

He had read that the area's heyday began in the 15th century, when the papacy returned to Rome. Throughout the Renaissance and Baroque eras, princes, popes, and cardinals settled here, as did the artists they commissioned to build and adorn lavish palaces, churches, and fountains.

He stood and began exploring the maze of narrow streets around the Pantheon, which had become the city's financial and political districts and was home to Parliament and the stock exchange. He marveled at the architecture.

As he walked, he was enticed by the aromas from the roasting meats and baked pastries of the shops. He stopped and sampled the salami made of wild boar as he drank in the atmosphere of the area. His taste buds were gratified by the juicy and aromatic sausage, and he detected a sweet hint of sherry in the marinade. As he nibbled, he watched the sausages being panseared in the kitchen, which extended outdoors.

He resumed his journey as a constant observer. In the tradition of their ancestors, artists painting in every medium from charcoal to oils to water colors formed two lanes of exhibits, luring tourists and the curious. He laughed as a green fluorescent Frisbee shot across the sky in front of the century-old Fontano Quattro, or Fountain of the Four Rivers.

It fed his hunger to learn more about this city. The wild boar had tickled his taste buds, and his stomach wanted more. Wandering the narrow streets, he found Il Giordano di Albino, a site recommended by one of his advisors. He quickly settled for a mouth-watering veal dish. He was surprised that in Italy the sauces never drowned the pasta.

He was also becoming enmeshed in the superstitions and culture of the Italians. He had recently made an overnight trip to Milan and knew it was one of the fashion capitals of the world. He glanced in windows filled with the latest trends bearing labels from Versace, Armani, and Gucci, to shoe stores selling

Ferragamo and Prada. He had written his mother that he had visited these shops and they both laughed about it when they spoke during his monthly phone call.

He appreciated his uncle's passion for opera, which led him to visit La Scala, where the elite had regular tickets to the operas. What made him so fond of this land was that amidst this wealth of culture, the people who lived here and in Rome were unpretentious and welcoming.

When he first arrived in the city, he was surprised at the traffic. It was like rush hour in most every other major city across the world. Twilight gradually melded into evening, and he came upon a sight that both inspired him and piqued his curiosity. He knew from his guide book that this was the Ponte Bridge, and from its perch up on the hill sat the museum of Castel Sant' Angelo, or the Castle of the Holy Angel. The bridge is adorned by a double row of angels, work of Bernini followers. It is from this view that the castle is best viewed. The lights from the dome were a halo of glory, painting the darkening September sky with an extrasensory quality. As he walked on the bridge, he noticed a group of tourists being led by a guide alongside the Tiber. He casually sauntered over to the side of the bridge, leaving the guide within earshot.

She began, "The Mausoleum of Hadrian, usually known as the Castel Sant Angelo, is a towering cylindrical building that was originally commissioned by the Roman Emperor Hadrian as his family's mausoleum. The building was later used by the popes as a fortress and castle, and is now a museum. Legend holds that the Archangel Michael appeared atop the mausoleum before Pope Gregory in the 6th century, sheathing his sword as a sign of the end of the plague of 590, thus lending the castle its current name."

She continued, "Built in 135 A.D. as a Roman emperor's mausoleum on the banks of the Tiber River, it is a mere fifteen-minute walk from Palazzo Farnese and Saint 'Andrea Della Valle. Now a national museum, it has displays of armor and piles of stone cannonballs and spooky passageways. For centuries it served as a state prison, and in the Middle Ages into the 1500s sheltered popes during some of Rome's many conflicts."

Captured by the beauty of the site, his mind wandered. He picked up the guide's speech in midsentence. "She was known as the beautiful patricide. Her tragic life came to symbolize the decadence and cruelty of 16th century Rome."

He eased closer, edging into the group. *One woman was a*

victim? Why would the city find her so important when giants had walked here? He had to learn more. He was rewarded.

"She was the daughter of Francesco Cenci, a Roman nobleman notorious for his viciousness and vice. He was well connected and avoided jail through bribery and favors, but he took his cruelty out on his family, especially his wife and daughter. In 1595, he imprisoned the two women in a castle outside of the city. He carried on with a number of mistresses. For three years the two women were abused, and the daughter claimed she was a victim of her father's incest."

Following her motion, the group followed. He ran to keep up. "The daughter convinced her two brothers to hire a killer and murder the father. Posing as servants, the two mercenaries accomplished the job by crushing the nobleman's skull as he slept, and threw his body off a balcony to make it appear as an accident. Beatrice's brother, Giacammo, had one of the killers eliminated so that he could not talk, but the other escaped. He was captured in Naples and told the truth at the family's trial."

He was completely absorbed in the story. He was hanging on every word and couldn't wait for the punch line. "Pope Clement VIII arrested the Cenci family. Everyone had great sympathy for the daughter because of her youth, beauty, and incest she had suffered." She stopped there as the group had met up with their bus. As they boarded she quickly added, "It didn't matter, because on September 11, 1599, she and her stepmother were beheaded. And ever since, they say on that date ..." They began boarding. "But the story goes on. However, I will finish the supernatural ending as we ride home."

Great. I'm hooked. Who was this woman? Why is she such a tragic figure that tour guides are still talking about her? Did she say the last name was Cenci? There had to be a record of this woman if the guide was talking about her. And she said supernatural ending. Was she a ghost? If so, might I see her? The library. I must check out this Cenci woman. And what happens on that day? It's only three days away."

The history book provided him with the answers. *Beatrice,* he thought. *How perfect.*

Just like Dante's guide in the Divine Comedy. A sudden stabbing pain shot across his forehead, climaxing in the back of his skull. He winced, blinked his eyes, and experienced an aura of faintly colored lights that swirled around him in shades of light blue and dark pink. He shook his head, closed his eyes and took a deep breath. *Anxiety,* he told himself. *Or renal fatigue from too much studying.*

The next day he went to the Barberini Palace and visited Guido Reni's portrait of Beatrice, said to be one of the city's most visited artworks. *She's beautiful.* Again, he was revisited by the swirling aura of lights and felt dizzy. *I haven't eaten,* he rationalized. And though he felt his equilibrium off kilter, he found his way to the snack bar and ordered a cappuccino coffee with a "cornetto," or croissant-style bread sweet.

As he consumed his breakfast, he continued reading the guide. Plays by Percy Bysshe Shelley and Albert Moravio were influenced by Beatrice's life. The Castel is featured prominently in Puccini's opera, "Tosca." An asterisk noted at the bottom of the page explained that superstition has it that every September 11 at night, Beatrice can be seen walking on the bridge of Sant' Angelo, carrying her head beneath her arm. Witnesses have testified that her spirit faithfully crosses the bridge on the anniversary of her death. For the people of Rome, she became a symbol of resistance against the arrogant aristocracy of her time, and another part of a legend arose.

While Giacomo was tortured with red-hot pincers, struck on the head with a bludgeon and quartered, the other brother, Bernardo, only twelve years old, was forced to watch the execution of his family and was condemned to life imprisonment. The two executioners who beheaded Beatrice and her mother, Lucrezia Petroni, Mastro Alessandro Bracca, and Mastro Peppe came to a tragic end. The first died thirteen days after the Cencis' death, while the second was stabbed to death at Porta Castello one month after Beatrice's death.

As he stood to leave, he felt an overwhelming sense of lightheadedness that forced him to resume his seat. He took several deep breaths and decided to go home to rest. Tomorrow was the eleventh, and he wanted to visit the bridge. He miraculously fell into a deep, undisturbed sleep.

After what he termed a good night's sleep of seven hours, he took a leisurely shower and visited his advisor. He was upbeat when he greeted him.

"Guess you were right, I'm really enjoying myself."

"Glad to hear that. You work hard at your studies and you deserve it. And the headaches? Are you still having them?"

"Occasionally, but less. Definitely less ... although..."

"Yes? "

"I've been seeing these lights, like an aura. Not all the time and they do go away."

"I think you are wise enough to know these very distinct symptoms. Perhaps it's time for a physical."

"Yes, I suppose."

He had researched his symptoms, but was in denial about the possibility of something so devastating as a tumor.

He pled with his advisor. "Can it wait until tomorrow? It's just a few hours, really. I've got a very important place to be tonight."

"Ah, you've met someone?"

"Yes, I guess you could say that. Anyway, I need to be on the Ponte Sant Angelo for an important meeting. I promise tomorrow I will check myself into the clinic, but it's probably a case of overwork."

"Justin, I must have it on the record that I recommend you be admitted now. I am not comfortable as a physician with your decision to delay this."

"Noted. I will be back tomorrow. You have my word."

The evening was particularly chilly for September. A cool breeze fanned over the bridge.

Shadows of the past writhed over the Eternal City. It was 11:45 p.m., and most of the tourists had gone. A few locals idled on the bridge in conversation or reverie. The teenagers, with their roaring cars and scooters, vacated the site.

He stood in the middle of the bridge, waiting. A smoky mist was forming at the far side of the bridge, closest to the Castle. He could just about make out the clothed figure of a woman. She was carrying something under her arm. Was it her head? Was this his Beatrice?

The pain in his head shot like an arrow, dulling his thinking process. His hand flew up to his head. *Not now,* he cried out. *Please, not now. I have to know!*

He did not recall what happened next until four hours later when he was confronted by his advisors and two other doctors. From his hospital bed he tried to get up, but his headache pulled him back down into the pillows.

"What was the last thing you remember?"

"It's incredible. I saw her. I saw the ghost of Beatrice Cenci. The legend is true. It's real!"

"Just lie back down and rest. You're going to need surgery. We'll prep you now. Then we can talk about the ghost."

The surgeon who was assigned his case interrupted.

"Excuse me doctor, but I'd like to ask him about the hair clip."

"Whatever this is about, make it quick."

The older doctor removed a tarnished hair clip from his pocket. "We found this in your clenched hand. Do you know where it came from?"

"I think I found it on the bridge. Do you think it was from the hair on the head she was carrying?"

"Who knows? Rest now. We'll be taking you in to remove the growth shortly."

"Do you believe his story?"

"I've heard the legend, we all have, but when you think of how this growth may be pressing on part of his brain, is it so far to assume it might be giving him visions as well?"

"Yes, I suppose so. Yet I remember reading that after she was killed, when the city was occupied by Napoleon's troops, the French soldiers stormed into the church of San Pietro in Montorio, where she was laid to rest. They smashed all the tombs, including Beatrice's, scattered her remains and even played with her decapitated skull as though it were a ball. So, with such a violent end, how can we rule out that he might really have seen the restless soul of this victim?"

NEVERMORE

"We are all tattooed in our cradles with the beliefs of our tribe; the record may seem superficial, but it is indelible. You cannot educate a man wholly out of the superstitious fears which were implanted in his imagination, no matter how utterly his reason may reject them."

Oliver Wendell Holmes, Sr.

Rays of sunlight reflected onto his body, giving a metallic purple shine to his black coat. He had been named Jim Crow in remembrance of the oldest raven ever to serve the Tower of London that had lived to the age of forty-four. As the breeze ruffled his feathers, he sat preening on his perch high above the legendary tower. His sharp eyesight and hearing had made him the newest leader of the other nine. With raptorial eyes, he scanned his domain. Mendel rustled nearby, showing off his impressive forty-six inch wingspan. Jim sensed danger and was on full alert. Instead of his usual "kaah," or cry for hunger, he emitted the distinct "quork," which triggered his sense of territorial danger.

His anxiety was justified. Four of his friends had gone and the daily routine had been interrupted. He sat waiting. And watching. He was not alone. All of England was on alert as the historical ravens went missing. This impacted on the psyche of the nation, for the raven had been as much a part of the British Empire's cultural heritage as the Crown Jewels, and far beyond the British Commonwealth, countries around the world have long attributed ominous symbolism to Jim's kind.

The Tower's colorful and violent history of murder and executions in the past has become an ironic footnote, since the site has become the bastion of safety for Great Britain. Jim had frequently heard the yeoman's stories and knew the tower was founded by William the Conqueror in 1066 and was enlarged over the years. It had served as a palace and fortress, prison, mint and menagerie, as well as repository of the royal crown jewels.

Jim scanned his domain. Next to him, Mendel, another raven, tagged blue for the other tower, grew restless. He too sensed impending danger.

From far below, the yeoman warders shared Jim's unease.

"All present and accounted for today," the elder guard named Smiley said.

"Aye," concurred his peer.

"The two replacements complete the count."

"Aye, at least for the time being."

Smiley, the senior yeoman warder, clad in his distinctive black and red uniform, peered into the sky above, in the back of his mind checking for unfamiliar planes. Terrorism had changed his job description and it was no understatement that danger lurked everywhere. The proof was in the heinous kidnapping of the ravens. Instead of an aircraft, he observed the disappearance of the sun, replaced by clouds that hung over the massive white tower and refused to budge. It was as though they were stuck in this air pattern and could not continue their journey across the heavens. When eventually they were pushed onward by a brief wind, the sky was vacant and grey.

"Something is very wrong," he observed. "I feel it in my bones. Never in my thirty-five years here has this happened, nor to my Dad during his forty years here. There is evil amongst us, and the ravens, and especially Jim, know it, too."

"I know," responded the other guard.

Smiley concluded, "Getting harder to give the speech about the legend, yet Raven Master Doyle says we must continue."

"Don't I know it. It's a worrisome time, it is."

Peg laid down the *London Times* and turned on the telly. The missing ravens were the topic everywhere these days. She felt sure, especially after she heard the Prime Minister, that it was connected to the terrorist bombings in London. She had never come close to such panic until a week ago, when she was indulging herself by attending an early show at the Piccadilly. The play was halted during the first act because of a bomb threat. Of course, British stiff upper lip and all, none of the patrons were upset. Everyone marched out calmly, the theater was searched, and it was concluded it was a false alarm. The audience returned and the play went on.

Newscasters reported another explosion in the theater district. It had become such a common facet of British life that the only ones who ran from the theater had been foreign tourists. If the frequent bombings had not bristled the hardy English people, the media seemed bent on pushing the angst in their faces. Just last week the *Times'* headline screamed, *"Tower raven found floating in the Thames."* Quick to jump on the media hype, the BBC ran a special about the legend of the ravens with an update on their mysterious kidnapping. The taping was also shown across the ocean in America.

The missing ravens had shattered the confidence of the locals, and everyone had an explanation for the tragedy and a solution to finding the culprit. These theories ran from mild to wild. Animal rights activists picketed before Parliament, demanding tightened security for the ravens. Historians pleaded for an intense investigation and limited access of the Tower to the public until the guilty party was found. This idea did not sit well with the Department of Tourism. "Many visitors make special plans to see the Tower. Without advanced notice of cancellation, many would be disappointed," their statement read.

Denial was also common. Politicians and some members of the House of Lords stated emphatically that it was not the Tower's ravens, since the wings of the drowned birds had not been clipped. Criminologists proposed the theory that the kidnappings were a distraction to take away attention from the Crown Jewels and was part of an elaborate plan to purloin the precious stones. This group called for additional guards.

Psychologists prattled on the telly nightly that the English people were easy targets because their superstitions about the ravens had taken complete control over their collective subconscious. "It is a modern world and superstitions have no purpose in it," they said. "Simply replace the birds and move on."

Steadfast in their beliefs, most people refused to "move on." Peg grew up with the legend and never thought there would be need to worry. After all, she concluded, the two World Wars had come and gone and the tower and England still stood, but now that the extremists seemed hell bent on destroying anyone and anything in a free nation, she wasn't so sure. And she felt that even though some humans were not concerned, the animal kingdom, which did not have the power of human speech, had instincts that served them well. She was sure the ravens' sensed imminent danger.

She knew there were always ten ravens at the tower. Since each of their wings were clipped, they cannot fly too far away, and it would seem the country was safe. Yet one by one the ravens were disappearing. The warders were desperately replacing the missing birds. The theft of the ravens was front page news. Riding the tubes, she overheard conversations amongst strangers about the mystery. It was debated over a basket of fish and chips and a pint at the local pub. Her coworkers were in a tither about what this could mean to the country. Many conjectured it was some crackpot with nothing better to do than harm the nation's revered birds. Alarmists attributed the captured ravens were being used in some bizarre occult ritual murders involving Satanists or witches that had evaded detection to date.

As Abdul paced the galleries of the British Museum on Russell Square, he reflected on the history of London's towers. Since he had been reassigned to the city it had been his only job. He got paid to learn the history, culture, and the British way of thinking.

"This was psychological warfare," he was told. On his way back to his hotel, he smoked another cigarette to calm his nerves. He did not like waiting, and it had been two days since he had heard from Samir, the mastermind of the mission.

Jim had ideas of his own. He sat with his wedge-shaped tail alert. Periodically, he opened his large, stout bill to caw. He was the leader because of his special instincts. He managed to avoid capture by the dark-faced man and he recognized his scent. The man was foul and wanted to harm the others. He was prepared. Though he had alerted the others, he could not be certain they would be effective in avoiding capture.

Within the week, Abdul had been assigned to capture another raven. It is said that a little knowledge may be a dangerous thing. Regardless of the terrorists' knowledge of British lore, they were ignorant of the fact that the ravens communicated and that they are considered the most intelligent of all birds. The men had not studied adequately as to the language of the birds that are able to imitate a variety of sounds, including the human voice. Abdul did not know that each of the ravens had a special talent. Thor, for example, was a very good mimic. On a quiet day he would repeat things the Raven Master has said to him with exactly the right words and vocal pitch. To the untrained and unfamiliar ear, it is hard to tell the difference between the master and Thor.

The ravens have distinct voices and their calls include guttural croaks, gurgling noises, and a sharp, metallic *"tock."* Their very cries could be interpreted to mean anything from hunger for their meals of rodents, insects, fruit, bird eggs, and grain, to their ability to mark their territory or alert humans to danger.

It is said that when a human is deprived of one of his senses, the body's other senses over compensate and become astute barometers of the lost sense. Similarly, stripped of their ability to fly because one wing is clipped, the ravens make do with their sharp beaks, which can tear through flesh instantly.

Abdul was familiar with the layout at the tower complex. For the third time this week he purchased his admission ticket and proceeded through the gate toward the tower. Previously, he had mentally mapped out the important sites of the tower area, noting the feeding area for the ravens. His disguise was a blond wig, complemented by clip earrings and a chain collar. The desired affect made a statement. For this visit, he had shaved his long scruffy beard and covered his shiny black hair with a non-descript baseball cap. His black sweatshirt matched his black pants and sneakers. He carefully found his way to the cages housing the ravens, where he was greeted by their gory dining ritual.

He observed an extra guard, no doubt an undercover Scotland Yard policeman, before the door to the kitchen area. From behind a large rock, he watched as the guard went in and out of the kitchen to get the food. As was their custom in late afternoon, they were feeding on raw meat and biscuits soaked in blood. As Abdul approached, Jim dropped the rabbit from his jaws and croaked. Carefully watching the guard enter the feeding shed, Abdul raced to the door, slammed it shut and shoved a large rock against it to wedge it closed. In this way, he eliminated further interference.

The birds were now all on high alert. Differentiated only by the differently colored bands on their legs, symbolizing which tower they inhabited, the group grew ominously silent. Thor edged closer to the edge of the cage, also abandoning his ration of fried bread from the Tower's kitchen.

"'Tis murder! Murder!" screamed Thor.

Ignoring the guard's persistent banging on the door, Abdul extracted the wire cutters from a bag on his belt and began cutting a hole into the lengthy cage. All ten of the ravens fled to the end of their cage. The hole was just big enough to allow Jim to wriggle his head out and sink his beak into the man's hand. The scene grew chaotic as one bird after the other managed to widen the gap and slide past Jim, freeing themselves from their prison. Jim held on tightly to the man's hand until all the ravens were free.

Mycroft, another of the larger ravens, replaced Jim's hold on the man's hand, allowing Jim to move across to the man's face. Sitting on the man's cheek, Jim craned his neck as he looked with black eyes into the would-be assailant's own guilty-yet-terrified eyes.

The still air was covered with elongated and pointed, pale-grayish-brown throat feathers that had been shed during the ravens' escape. Their flight to the ground, where they lay like petals during a funeral procession, was tribute to the violence the tower has known for generations. Countless tortures, murders, and executions stain the buildings and the grounds.

Jim patiently waited for the others to join him, and one by one they tackled their prey. Each of the ravens pecked their beaks into the man's flesh, drawing numerous sources of blood. Jim paced up to the side of the man's temple and quickly drove his beak into the vulnerable eye until it was removed. When he finished, he began working on the second.

Abdul's cries were unheard, so loud was Thor in his accusation of "Murder! Murder!" As the senior warders came upon the scene, Mycroft was parading around with the long, pink, slithery tongue that once belonged to Abdul. Abdul's body, sans eyes and tongue, was ravaged with dozens of puncture wounds, compliments of the ravens who now sat quietly in a "V"- shaped formation behind Jim.

Smiley and Wendell looked at each other, their faces registering their shock. Finally, Smiley ordered Wendell to get another cage for the birds.

"Shouldn't we open the door for the sergeant first?"

"Not yet. It is enough to have we two as the only witnesses. Go get another cage first."

"But what do we do with the body? Should we call the police?" Wendell asked.

"We already have a member of the police here, remember? You heard Thor. He murdered the ravens.

"Yes, but ..."

"This is a place of justice and revenge, Wendell. And more times than not, the law has not been brought into consideration. Just think of all of Henry's wives and the blood baths that were never fully expiated. You should full well know this. Remember the history here."

"You mean-?" Wendell said with incredulity. "Are you saying that we should-?"

"All I am saying now is that the ravens will dine well tonight, Wendell. Yes, indeed. And as the days go on, I think the havoc that has threatened the towers and England will bring us yet one more legend to perpetuate."

THE SPEAR OF DESTINY

"It is the customary fate of new truths to begin as heresies and to end as superstitions."

Aldous Huxley

"Do come in, Herr Hitler."

The invitation by Dietrich Eckert leads into a windowless space with black walls. A sparse scattering of candles flicker from atop the fireplace mantle. The focal point of the area is the floor, upon which is painted a blood-red pentagram with various unfamiliar symbols. A large round table fills the opposite side of the Spartan room and is surrounded by thirteen high-backed chairs. Observing his guest drawn to the diagram, Eckert explains, "It is to direct forces and energies that represent the Thule Society and our observation of Satanism." This is spoken with a sly smile so malignant in its countenance that the young man momentarily shivers.

He nevertheless moves forward. "You should know exactly what we are about, Herr, before you commit to join us. We perform certain rituals of a sexual nature and include animal sacrifice, blood scourging, and more. Should any of this repulse you or intimidate you in any way, you may leave now."

"No, I am not afraid."

"Good. Then let me add that to enhance our minds we frequently utilize certain substances. I find morphine quite useful. Is there a problem with this?

"None, sir."

"Fine. The others will be here in a few moments. Are you ready for the initiation?

"Yes," the young man timidly responds.

"Follow me." The two proceed through a secreted passage that leads to a lower level in the building. A variety of tools are spread out across a long table. A chain apparatus hangs from the wall. The young man espies whips and manacles, and is temporarily off balance.

He is forced to stand naked before the faceless others, who are huddled around their tables. The room is pitch, like an abyss, save for a sparse glimmering of tapers atop another fireplace. The glowing coals in the hearth settle. Luminous red sparks fly up the chimney, eager to escape from the ritual. The smoldering wood emits a thick smoke, which stings his eyes. A chair is found and he is tied with his arms behind his back. His feet are laced together to the bottom rung of the chair. One of the members rises from his seat and moves toward him. The man bends over, staring Hitler in the face, and touches his nether region. He squirms with disdain but says nothing. *I am being tested,* he thinks.

Herr Dietrich reads aloud, "I have been annunciated with a vision to prepare the anti-Christ to conquer the world and lead the Aryan race to glory. As head of the Thule Society, I ask the group: Do you believe in the coming of a German messiah that will restore Germany after its defeat during World War I?"

"We do," the others who have risen intone. "And further, do you believe that the anti-Christ to whom I refer is none other than the man who sits humbled before you, known on this earth as Adolph Hitler?"

"We do."

The focus now turns to Hitler. "In this year of 1919, Adolph Hitler, do you swear to fulfill your duties as a member of the Thule Society and endure whatever rituals are deemed necessary to comply with your role as the future Anti-Christ?"

"I do."

"Do you, of your own free will, agree to pursue whatever means required to mete out justice to those in the way of your attaining the goal of creating an Aryan master race?"

"I do."

"Do you believe that you are a descendent of the Aryans, a race of Caucasian 'supermen' who lived nearly a million years ago?"

"I do."

"Do you agree, of your own volition, to submit to any and all rituals that are deemed appropriate to ready your body and mind for your future leadership?"

"I do."

He hears the whip lashing in the background. With the first assault on his body, he blacks out. In the days that follow, he is filled with supernatural hatred and venom. The acts of perversion to which he has submitted has instilled a determination that is steely cold and cruel toward others.

Within the year, the young malcontent wanders the streets of Vienna, searching for a means to his succession as the Anti-Christ. The magnificence of his surroundings eludes him. Oblivious to the grand Gothic architecture of St. Stephen's Cathedral, the aroma of the Sacher Torte's baking at the Hotel Sacher, and the romantic horse-drawn carriage rides, he has only one thing on his mind: his destiny.

His initial meeting with a journalist and playwright has shaped his thinking. He knows he will eventually alter history, and so he makes his way with determination and purpose to his mentor's temporary residence to learn more about the grand plan. He knows no religion and is vulnerable to alternate philosophies that promise ultimate power. He has no compassion; his is a heart of darkness. His strong will and recent dabbling into the Occult Thule Society, headed by Eckart, has helped form the core of his philosophy which will dictate his actions.

He is ready for the next step: a visit with Madame Helena Blavatsky, known as the priestess of the occult. Legend had it that as a child of four she had withdrawn her protective powers over a child, resulting in his drowning. Born of Russian nobility, she was familiar with superstitions and the supernatural at an early age. It was common knowledge amongst those in the Thule Society that paranormal beings could be placated, or even controlled, by people like Helena. On the night of her birthday, the servants would carry the little girl around the house and stables while sprinkling holy water and repeating magical incantations to appease the *domovoy,* a goblin in the form of an old man who lived behind the stove and played tricks whenever displeased.

Hitler is taken aback by the woman's large hypnotic steely blue eyes and forceful stare. Rarely has he had the occasion to meet a woman so bold, yet he is intensely aware that her approval is key to his success. As head of the House of Theosophy, she is a key leader to the drive to the New World Order. He knows of her involvement in Satan worship. He has memorized the lines from her book, "The Secret Doctrine :Lucifer represents ... Life ... Thought ... Progress ... Civilization ...Liberty ... Independence ... Lucifer is the Logos ...the Serpent, the Savior." It has become his Bible, as it sits on his nightstand and is what he reads before retiring each evening.

Blavatsky, writing through Tibetan Masters, also wrote "Isis Revealed," and from her "Secret Doctrine," he derived a deep malice for all Jews, considering them to be an inferior race. He is confident that as inferiors, they threaten the purity of the German people. He is honored to be in Blavatsky's presence. He feels an instant allegiance to her.

"Please, sit, Herr Hitler."

As he takes his seat, he notices the attendance of Eckhart. It is apparent they have prepared another session for him, and as if on cue, his body becomes numb. He must steel himself for whatever torture they have in mind, for he has come to accept that this is a part of his initiation to become the Anti-Christ. This includes his vision to lead Germany and unite the world under his leadership for one thousand years.

"Madame Blavatsky, may I introduce our long-awaited savior, Adolph Hitler."

The powerful woman speaks directly to him. "Herr Hitler, you need to become aware of your body. Power is wired through your physical body and you need to control it for your own use. This is known as 'transcendent consciousness,' which will require meditations and chemical substances, so critical to opening up your Pineal Gland, or the Third Eye of Eastern Mysticism," Madame Blavatsky says.

"Do you understand?"

"Yes."

"And in what ways have you ensured the purification of your body?"

"I eat no red meat, neither do I consume alcohol or beer, and I do not smoke."

"Commendable. At least we do not have to prepare you from the very beginning of purging your physical self. Very well, let us begin."

Hitler soon learns of the vehicle which will grant him the power to lead the revolution in the name of a Biblical relic: *The Spear of Destiny*. With Eckert's guidance, Hitler has studied the occult meanings underlying Wolfram Von Eschenbach's 13th century Grail Romance, "Parsival," which first brought to his attention the talismanic powers of the spear.

Hitler has been an avid reader. Particularly of the occult genre. The lance, he knows, is mentioned in St. John's Gospel, and has passed through many persons since. He learns that a thousand years ago when Jesus hung in agony on the cross, a Roman soldier stabbed his side with a spear. The blood that stained the tip of the spear was deemed holy. Legend has it that this act of cruelty and violence against the Prince of Peace imbibed a supernatural power onto the spear. The belief is that the spear gave all who possessed it a great power that was potent enough to conquer the world. Conversely, when the spear was lost, it brought death. For centuries, people have believed in the power of talismans considered to possess supernatural or magical powers that will be endowed upon its owner.

He wants validation. He requires proof beyond the superstitions. Historical references confirmed his hopes. For more than one thousand years, the spear was a symbol of power to the emperors of the Holy Roman Empire. As early as 615 A.D. the relic was reportedly seen in Jerusalem. The names of its owners included Constantine the Great and Emperor Charlemagne, who lived and slept within reach of the spear and attributed forty-seven battle victories to its powers. In the late 1700s it was moved to Vienna. In all, forty-five emperors claimed the spear as a possession.

Now it is his turn. Hitler becomes obsessed with the spear and resolves at all costs to obtain it from its display case in the Hapsburg Treasure House Museum. It is 1920, and he has come to Munich, forging his way through the crowds in the Marienplatz, ignoring the hourly spectacle of the Rathaus-Glockenspiel, where tourists from around the world come to enjoy the amusement of the forty-three bells and thirty-two life-sized figures that circle the tower. He has no time for such nonsense. *This tradition is for fools,* he thinks. His time is better served.

His destination is the Hofbrauhaus, Platzl 9, where between beer and salted pretzels amidst the gay music of the accordion players, he meets with others of his mind. The young boys of Germany are easily influenced, and the beer helps in nurturing their sense of nationalistic pride. These meetings quickly become rousing affairs. He realizes the necessity of enlisting the support and favor of these young men. This is the start of his recruitment for his army.

Hitler has learned well how to manipulate people. He becomes a master at psychologically influencing his army, and on February 24th, he proclaims the twenty-five theses of the National Socialist program which reconstitutes the German Workers Party as the National Socialist German Workers Party, aka – The Nazi Party.

By the age of thirty-three, he is totally possessed by the Evil Hierarchies of Spirits, and prepares to take the leadership of the National Socialist Party. Fortified by his occult beliefs and the prophecy of his own leadership, he attracts a discontented people. He inflicts a sense of elitism upon the easily swayed people. Promoting a race of white, blond-haired, blue-eyed stock of people in 1933, his party becomes the top choice of the German people, who have lost faith in the parties of the political center because of the great hardships during the 1920s and the Great Depression of 1929. The people want change and a strong leader, and Hitler fits the bill. He becomes Chancellor.

On his meteoric rise to power, he never forgets his quest for the Spear of Destiny. It is foremost in his mind as he plots his destiny, and although rumors arc rampant that there is more than one spear, his focus is on the one which rests in Vienna.

"They try to trick me," he concludes. His opportunity to obtain the inscribed spear of silver and gold comes in 1938, when he annexes Austria, invades the Hofmsueum, and takes the coveted holy lance. Those who witness his discovery note his reverence before it. Some describe it as a religious experience when they heard these words: "I feel as though it has always been mine. At some point in earlier history I possessed it, and now it is once again mine. The prophecy will be fulfilled. Of this there is no doubt."

His psychological control results in an army of horror upon the world as he leads the Nazi party to fiendish acts of depravity on humanity in search of his quest for a white, blond haired, blue-eyed stock of people. As he invades Poland, he advances World War II. Throughout the bloodbath of his leadership, he remembers his pledge to the Thule Society in utilizing the spear to capture the Jews. Within the terrors of the concentration camps, he sanctions surgeries without anesthesia. Many victims suffer intense agony, mutilation, and permanent disability. These Jews suffer the effects of poisons, drugs, ice water, sterilization, and starvation. Those are the lucky ones. For some it's a direct march to the showers – the gas chambers. It matters little to Hitler, for he is the Anti-Christ and he will advance his race and his position in the New World Order. And of course, he's got the spear, which he believes will fortify his quest.

But by October 1944, success has shifted to the Allied side. He moves the spear, along with the stolen art collections, to a specially constructed underground vault that will protect it from heavy bombing. It is hidden along with thousands of art treasures his armies pilfered during the battles and invasions he led. The art seizures in France alone total 21,903 objects from 203 collections.

On April 30, 1945 at 2:10 p.m., advancing American forces of the third army under General George S. Patton take possession of the vault and the spear. Hitler's reign of terror has ended, and eighty minutes later, he dies by his own hand in a bunker in Berlin. To some, he has fulfilled the prophecy of ownership of the spear of destiny. When he had it in his possession, he won the battles of the war. When he left it to hide it, he lost the powers it bestowed upon him and the Allied forces assumed control. Others say Hitler was not so much looking for power, but money, and only wanted it for financial gain, as many of the other art treasures he had commandeered during the war.

Though Patton wants to keep the spear, it is ordered to be

returned to the Austrians.

"Mr. President, sir, we have the spear in our possession. What is your command?"

"Return it to the people of Austria," said President Franklin D. Roosevelt.

It sits now in the Hofburg Museum.

THE WAYS OF THE WENDIGO

"Fear is the main source of superstition, and one of the main sources of cruelty. To conquer fear is the beginning of wisdom."

Bertrand Russell

The weather for northern Minnesota looked grim. The moisture-laden atmosphere matched the darkening clouds that filled the winter skies above the Beaver State. Anyone who lived here for any significant amount of time could predict the oncoming storm; and it would pack a powerful punch.

Tim Lockwood turned the volume on his television to its maximum setting. "The snow should develop from south to north across the region this afternoon and evening. The heaviest snowfall should occur from tonight through all day tomorrow. Snowfall rates of two to three inches per hour are likely. With a northeast wind of 30-45 mph, visibilities will drop to zero, with considerable blowing and drifting of the snow. Travel and commerce across the warning area are expected to be severely impacted by heavy snow and significant drifting will make clearing of the roads nearly impossible."

Tim turned off the television and pulled on his heavy waterproof hiker boots. He had been waiting for this forecast for weeks now, and he wanted to take advantage of it. He had already received the call from the Department of Sanitation where he worked that his services would not be required today. The logic was to wait out the accumulation before cleaning up. This was fine with him, as he had been hoping for such weather when he would have called in sick anyway. He loved to forage the woods and this was the country for it. It was in the heart of the cold winter that he felt at one with the forest of evergreens, pines, and firs that proliferated the northern landscape of the Leech Lake Indian Reservation.

From the bottom kitchen cabinet, he pulled out a large plastic tablecloth and spread it out evenly across the floor. Next, he retrieved a large yellow manila envelope from his dresser drawer, spilled the contents into his palm and pocketed the items into his dark grey parka. He pulled his mask over his head, topped it with a fur trapper's hat, slung his weather-worn backpack over his shoulder and concluded his attire with thermal weatherproof gloves. The hunt was on.

It took the coroner's office two days to sift through the shreds of torn ligaments and half chewed flesh and bone found on the forest floor before confirming thc corpse was that of a child. It was gruesome fodder for the media, which, after receiving numerous and almost always anonymous letters, issued banner headlines that blazoned, *"Is Wendigo back?"* on the front pages of the local and county newspapers. Other papers capitalizing on the salacious nature of the crime were more cutting edge: *Blood thirsty Wendigo Kills Child.* Of course the death of a child, particularly in such a hideous and savage manner, would always make the headlines, but the connection to the Wendigo triggered fear and panic within the public and the publishers of papers like *The Sentinel, The Journal,* and *The Free Press,* who knew that paranoia sold papers. Not to go with such a blatant headline was just not good business sense.

Everyone who lived in this region was familiar with the superstition about the cannibalistic Wendigo that roamed the northern United States and Canada. Insulating skepticism prevailed as long as there were no reports of missing children. Here in Minnesota's frozen land, it was viewed through the prism of this biting cold winter: a supernatural essence that devoured human children. Though no one had recently claimed to see the monster-man, there had been clues. The bear-like claws broken off into the child's flesh was just one example of a non-human killer. The brutal wounds, indicative of skin being ripped with a strength and vehemence unknown to a mortal, substantiated the rumors of the Wendigo as the culprit. It was also easier to believe that no human could be capable of such extreme violence and destruction.

A spirit of the woods, the Wendigo has been reported for decades amongst campers and hunters in the shadowy forest of the area. Sketches of the creature varied; everyone agreed its appearance was emaciated. Some asserted it has an ashy gray skin tone with deep-set eyes. All concurred it reeked of rot and decay from consuming human flesh, and what terrified the masses was that its rampages were not a one-time occurrence. A single killing would not suffice. Once the monster began its lust it could only find fulfillment with excessive sprees of bloodshed.

The origin of the monster has been traced back to the Ojibwa/Saulteaux, the Cree and the Innu/Naskapi/Montagnais tribes. Though descriptions varied somewhat, common to all these cultures was the concept that the Wendigo is malevolent, anti-social, and cannibalistic, possessing great spiritual power, and its prey was almost always children. The monster was almost always associated with the winter, the north, and coldness, as well as with famine and starvation.

Tim knew all about the Wendigo. The fact that he stood only

five feet tall, had an extremely wide girth, and paunch to match, and was nearly bald and the Wendigo was a giant of fifteen feet in stature made it the object of his fascination and admiration. He marveled at what it would be like to be feared instead of being the brunt of everyone's jokes. He had tolerated such treatment as a child, but vowed never to be debased like that again. He envied the power and strength of the feared beast.

But what he really liked about the fiend was that whenever it consumed another person, in most cases a child, it would increase in size in proportion to the meal it had just devoured. Since the body accommodated its intake, it could never really be completely full. He had read about one camper who had resorted to cannibalism because he was starving, and after being rescued could only abide human flesh.

The creature's physical description varied. He had read Native American stories that described the beast as having protruding, yellow, glowing eyes that roll around in blood and an overly long tongue. Reports indicated the creature's gigantic maw was filled with long, needle-like teeth. It's hissing, it was said, could rival the wind velocity of a storm and could be heard for miles. This, he thought, was likely an exaggeration. Its breath reeked of rancid meat and decay. There were also accounts of the monster having a sallow, yellowish complexion, and a body covered with matted, mangy hair.

The paws, legend had it, ended in talons a foot or more in length, while its feet measured three feet in length ending with a single long dagger-like nail used to slash and tear its prey. This description captivated Tim, who was uneducated, unrefined, and mountain-man like in his inner savagery. What he lacked in sophistication he made up for with an affinity for young children, where the gentle side of his nature was revealed. He played well with his nephews, though he knew they complained to their parents he seemed overly touchy and had the weird habit of sniffing them. He also knew his brother George would dismiss any perversity they implied, thereby allowing no suspicions to be cast upon him.

The wind picked up in its ferocity as the ice pellets drove through the storm, creating an eerie howling sound that sent most residents indoors. With the publication of the news of the dead child, it was not the weather conditions that prompted their hibernation. They were not sure if the sounds are indeed the call of nature, or the beast known as the Wendigo.

Earlier in December, the residents who believed the legend examined the trees in the area. Using ladders, they climbed as high as possible to discern any large pots hiding in branches. They knew that these pots could be filled with human remains, and were stashed by the Wendigo in preparation for a long winter ahead.

The follow up on the child's death spawned additional coverage by the local television networks, which despite the weather conditions, were able to operate on their well-powered generators. On one of the talk shows, Dr. Leonard Rimes tried to assuage the panic-stricken people of the town by explaining the "Wendigo Psychosis." The author of several books on the subject, the psychology professor explained to the host, Mort Evans, "It all goes back to the winter of 1878, when a Cree trapper named Swift Runner and his family was starving. His eldest son died. With lack of any speedy transportation to the nearest food supplies at a Hudson Bay Company Post, a good twenty-five miles away, he went mad and butchered his wife and remaining children and ate them."

"Wow, that's some story, Dr. Rimes."

"If I may continue, he confessed and was executed at Fort Saskatchewan. This act of pure cannibalism was really a resort by someone who was suffering from Wendigo Psychosis, and became a homicidal cannibal."

"Gee, doctor, I've heard of cannibalism in the jungle, but here in the north of Minnesota?"

"There have been credible eyewitness accounts by Algonquians and by westerners as proof that it was a factual historical phenomenon."

"Are you saying that perhaps this latest killing and mutilation of a child is not the work of a Wendigo, but rather the result of a distorted mind suffering from this Wendigo Psychosis?"

"I'm merely presenting another possibility to consider in this mystery. Ethnographers, psychologists, and anthropologists have hotly debated the controversy during the 1980s. It's like the Big Foot Legend. How real are these creatures? Could the legend have been created for or interpreted as a warning against cannibalism? A Wendigo allegedly made an appearance near the town of Rosesu in Northern Minnesota in the late 1900s through the 1920s. There are believers and there are non-believers, but the one concern is to find out who or what committed this crime and to stop any future violence."

"Thank you for your insight, doctor. When we return from commercial break we will be speaking with Bob Albert, an historian from these parts."

"Mr. Albert, nice to have you with us."

"Thanks for having me."

"Our previous guest detailed some of the legends that have sprung up around these parts in the 19th century. I understand you can fill our audience in on additional stories?"

"Yes. As your previous guest indicated, Native Americans actively believed in, and searched for, the Wendigo. One of the most famous Wendigo hunters was a Cree Indian named Jack Fiddler. He claimed to kill at least fourteen of the creatures in his lifetime, although the last murder resulted in his imprisonment at the age of eighty-seven. In October 1907, Fiddler and his son, Joseph, were tried for the murder of a Cree Indian woman. They both pleaded guilty to the crime, but defended themselves by stating that the woman had been possessed by the spirit of a Wendigo and was on the verge of transforming into one entirely. According to their defense, she had to be killed before she murdered other members of the tribe."

"Mesmerizing."

"Yes, and frightening as well. There are still many stories told of Wendigos that have been seen in northern Ontario, near the Cave of the Wendigo, and around the town of Kenora, where a creature has been spotted by traders, trackers, and trappers for decades. There are many who still believe that the Wendigo roams the woods and the prairies of northern Minnesota and Canada. Whether it seeks human flesh or acts as a portent of coming doom is anyone's guess."

"Can you tell us how does one kill a Wendigo? I mean, is there a way that you know?"

"They allegedly do have a few weaknesses. It is said that it can be killed by iron, steel, or silver. Almost like a vampire, the best way is to shatter its heart with a silver stake and then dismember its body."

"That's hard to believe in today's world. It's like we're talking about superstitious creatures back two centuries ago. Dr. Rimes attributes a lot of the killings to a human suffering from Wendigo Psychosis, but it sounds as though you believe there really is a monster - or monsters – out there killing for food."

"I have no concrete proof of that, but I can say that before you start to doubt that it exists, remember that the stories and legends of this fearsome creature have been around since before the white man walked on these shores. The legends had to have gotten started somehow, didn't they?"

"Indeed, Mr. Alberts. Certainly a possibility."

With the conclusion of the interview, Mort added his own two cents. "Listeners, your intrepid host has done some of his own research as well. Apparently, the legend has drawn attention from around the world. Back in the 50,s an English novelist and short-story writer named Algernon Henry Blackwood wrote a story about the Wendigo. Since he was a member of The Ghost Club based in London, the story was a tale of horror. I guess every facet of culture has their own spin on the Wendigo. All we can do is hope for the best. And now the latest on the weather."

The Rayburn children were ecstatic with the snow day. Not only did it mean no school, but it was a chance to play outdoors. Their cabin was located on a steep incline that during the winter was perfect for tobogganing. They begged and pleaded with their mother for just one quick run down the slope, after which they would stay indoors and read books – especially if mom promised to make them some hot chocolate. Reluctantly, Deb Rayburn agreed. She double checked her three boys were bundled tightly against the chill wind, wrapping a bright red scarf around each of their necks before releasing them into the snow storm. She had every intention of letting them play for only fifteen or twenty minutes, and then the phone rang.

Deb lost track of the time, and when she looked out the window she observed a complete whiteout. Visibility was zero. Even the black skull caps on the boys' heads were not to be seen.

She ran out the door, forgoing her own coat and screamed, "Boys! Boys!" Her heart was wildly fluttering. Miraculously, two figures with their red scarves wildly blowing in the wind, marched slowly out of the storm up the hill, minus the toboggan. Each step was an apparent struggle as they fought the pelting snow and ice, struggling with their balance against the ferocious winds while climbing the hill. It impeded their rapid progress. She waited for the third and youngest son. He never came.

Tim returned late that night, totally exhausted but filled with pride and accomplishment. It had taken him longer than he thought, but he had been successful. From his drenching backpack he pulled out his prey, slamming it onto the wooden cutting board atop the kitchen island. He wasted no time in skinning the meat from the bone and stopped only long enough to remove his coat, which made for clumsy movement. From one of the cabinets above the stove, he grabbed a bag of flour, salt and pepper. Pouring oil into the iron skillet, he added chopped onions and then waited for the pan to heat. When it began to sizzle and spatter over the stove, he carefully placed the meat into the hot oil.

The remaining upper half of the prey he hung with a steel hook atop the rafter. The metal snare was smeared with dried blood, so there was no dripping onto the plastic tablecloth on the floor, yet from previous experience he thought it best to be prepared. He was glad, since the freezing snow was doing enough of a job on the floor as it melted onto the wood below. He ignored it and turned on the television.

A frisky blond anchor woman was reading the headlines. "Next is a Minnesota couple who have lost their young son in a whiteout. We've got a live interview with Sheriff Augustus La Pierre, who says he'll hold off an extensive search until the snow decreases and the wind dies down. Here now is the sheriff."

"It's just too hard to see anything right now. We are all on high alert and just as soon as the weather permits we will be out there twenty-four hours a day until we find the boy. We have no intentions of abandoning the search. It's heartbreaking to have to wait, but we are left no real choice."

An officer standing behind the sheriff nudged his superior, handing him a red scarf. La Pierre continued, "I'm afraid the only thing we have located thus far is this scarf, which has been identified as belonging to the missing boy."

The anchor concludes, "The child's parents are putting out a monetary reward for the safe return of their son." A snapshot of a tow-headed boy of perhaps six flashed across the screen. This was followed by a tearful middle-age woman clinging to her husband as she pled for help from anyone who would listen.

Tim snickered. *Mothers these days just don't watch their kids,* he thought. *All it takes is just one minute to look the other way. So much can happen in so little time. Bet she changes her parenting skills now.*

He returned to the stove and, using a spatula, flipped the slab of meat onto its other side for browning. From the refrigerator he removed an icy cold beer. It was the perfect complement to the meat. He sat down and finished his meal, smacking his lips with satisfaction. Although he was bone tired, he forced himself to flay the rest of the meat, wrap it in brown paper and pack it in the freezer. He would be ready for the long winter ahead.

MOMENTO MORI

"There is a faculty in man that will acknowledge the unseen. He may scout and scare religion from him; but if he does, superstition perches near."

Joseph Sheridan Le Fanu,
The Haunted Baronet and Others: Ghost Stories 1861-70

"Daniel, can you hear me? Stop staring at the ceiling and ignoring me. Daniel! Daniel!"

"What?" the voice shrieks.

"You don't have to scream. Everyone will hear you."

"So? What difference does that make? Sometimes you are such a nag, Nigel. I don't have to answer you. Does that ever occur to you?"

Nigel pauses to think. "But eventually you always do."

"Yes, sadly. But maybe I won't anymore."

"What does that mean?"

"What do you think it means?" he taunted his brother with this melodramatic affectation.

"That you're going to play that stupid game again." He sighs loudly, gesticulating with his hands in frustration.

"What game is that, Nigel?"

Nigel's clenched fists hammer against his thighs. The action adds further irritation to his already itchy legs, which are allergic to the scratchy tweed of his trousers. In a controlled, but angry voice, he explains, "The one where you always make me mad."

"Oh, *that* game. You're very good at that, aren't you?"

Nigel smiles, narrowing his eyes like a cat. "Yes. Yes, I am."

"It never has taken much to make you mad, Nigel. All anyone has to do is to want something that you want."

The conversation comes to an abrupt halt. Daniel is still staring up at the ceiling, in no apparent hurry to move. It frustrates Nigel, who nervously paces about the room the two share, finally coming to rest on his twin bed.

"Daniel? Daniel!" Nigel's rising panic was easily discerned.

"I'm still here. Why are you always so mean, Nigel?"

Nigel smiles again. He subconsciously thrusts his chest out, in silent acknowledgment of what his brother has just said. "Do you really think I am?"

"Quite definitely. And you are very much aware of it, and so are mean as often as you can arrange to be. Remember the time you strung that wire across the second step and Rosie tripped and broke her arm?"

Nigel giggles. "That was hilarious."

Daniel continues, "She hurt her collarbone. And you blamed me."

"Yes, and I got away with it." His voice brimmed with

unconcealed joy.

"Then there was the time that you put that awful Castor Oil in Aunt Jane's tea."

"Ha! Did you see her face? That was priceless!"

"You got away with that, too."

"Yes. Yes I did. What great fun."

"Do you know why?"

Nigel rises from the bed and walks to his brother's side.

"I said, do you want to know why I took the blame for all the things you have done? Why I never protested my innocence?"

Nigel is still now. He runs his hand through his smooth blond hair and looks into the mirror that hangs between their two beds. He is disappointed to see not only his own reflection, but that of his brother as well. He thinks, *I'm so sick of seeing you everywhere I am.*

"I'm going to tell you now. I've been holding back, but now I've decided I'm going to tell you my secret."

"What secret? How could you hide a secret from me?" A snaking live wire of dread ignites a knot in his stomach.

"I know you think we are always connected. That you can finish my sentence before I speak it. That we pretty much know what the other is going to say before it is said. But I've found a way to keep a secret from you."

"I don't believe you. You can't do that. And even if you are, I could do it too if I wanted to. I can do anything I put my mind to." His face reddens with anger.

"Really? I have been keeping a secret for years now, and it's about you. And you never guessed."

"What kind of a secret?"

"Nigel, you were a mistake. Mother and father planned to have me, and when you came after me, well, it was a great shock and disappointment to them. *I* was wanted. *You* were *not.* They had no idea we were twins. And since I was born first, I was the one they were expecting."

Nigel stands before his brother, mouth agape. This was the first he had heard this story. His bravado quickly returns. "So? Big deal."

Daniel continues, "I'm surprised that is your only comeback. Perhaps it is too great a shock at the moment. Given time, however, I'm sure you can think up a barb to hurl at me. You always do. But Nigel, I want you to know that I know that you are evil. And you, dear brother, will burn in hell. I, on the other hand, am headed for heaven."

"How do you know that?"

"I have my means of knowing many things that you don't."

"That's a lie. You are making this up. Take it back or I'll..."

"You'll what, Nigel? Pull my hair? Hide my watch? Turn my friends against me? Blame me for one of your pranks? Or maybe, you will steal my medicine again? You know, the one that would have healed me faster. You've pulled these tricks many times before. Nothing you do to me or to anyone else can surprise me. In fact, I've become quite bored with your behavior. It is stagnant."

"Shut up. Just shut up!" Nigel's chin juts forward aggressively. He scrambles for a comeback. Beads of sweat plaster his forehead, dampening his combed hair.

"The truth hurts." An unnatural quiet reigns over the room. *Is that a smile on Daniel's face?* he wonders. The sound of the ticking hallway clock is magnified by the deadly silence in the room.

"What are they doing now, Nigel?"

"Why do you care?"

"I want to know. Why can't you tell me?"

"They're preparing for the family portrait."

"Oh, yes. Like the one we did last year for Aunt Violet. Well, then, how do I look?"

"Just like you always look, Daniel. Like a copy of me. Like a fake copy. But just wait until this portrait is done ...."

"Stop right there, little brother. I am the original. I came first. You are the copy, second best, not good enough. Not wanted. An uninvited guest, as it were."

Nigel's left hand is balling into a fist. He wants so much to punch his brother, but he can't, because it will ruin the portrait and this is one thing he cannot blame on his brother.

His response is feeble, "You just wait till after the picture."

"Oh, I'll be waiting, Nigel. I'll be waiting for you."

From the hallway, their mother calls out: "Nigel, are you with your brother?"

"Yes, mother. We're waiting for the portrait."

Unearthly quiet dominates the room. No more words are to be exchanged. In the next room, the soft rushing of their mother's black silk frock can be heard. She will stand behind the twins in the picture, grasping the long cuffs of lace fringe fastened with two buttons and loops around her wrists. It is a nervous habit she has had for as long as they can remember. Nigel could picture her brushing her hair up into its severe style, so common among other matrons of the day.

In this age of Queen Victoria, such photographs was becoming de rigueur. It was fashionable to arrange for a photographer to actually come into the house and capture the images of the entire family for posterity. *For remembrance,* his mother had stressed. The invention of the Carte de Visite, which enabled multiple prints to be made from a single negative, meant that images could be sent to distant relatives as well. Their mother indicated she had intentions of sending one to her family in Sussex.

Their mother descends the stairs, barking at the housekeeper.

"Martha, are the biscuits done yet?"

As she scurries out of the kitchen, black wax dried onto her hands, the frantic housekeeper responds, "Yes, madam. I've finished wrapping them in the paper and I'm now sealing them."

"Good. Don't forget the mirrors when you've finished. And the velvet squares?"

"I've unpacked them. I'll get to it after the mirrors."

"Have the flowers arrived yet?"

"No, madam. I expect they'll be here any time now."

"I hope so. We have a protocol to follow."

"Yes, madam.

Her husband joins her. Softly touching his shoulder she confides, "I'm a nervous wreck. Thank God I have these details to see to, Gerald."

He takes her hand and pats it gently. "It will be fine, dear."

She turns her attention back to her servant."Everything must be up to standard, Martha. There is only one opportunity to get this right. Have you seen to the clocks?"

Martha looks at the large grandfather clock and notes the wording above the face: tempus fugit, "time flies." She acknowledges her mistress, "Yes, Madam."

Though it was emotionally exhausting for the family, it was nevertheless important to have the house up to order for the occasion. The clocks, the flowers, and the food were an inherent part of the ritual. It was important to be well-dressed for the portrait. The photographer had many other such photographs to take. Houses all over their district were on the list. There would be just this one opportunity for the family to be as one before they all moved on, and so Nigel brushes his suit as his twin, Daniel, rests in bed.

"Oh, dear, I do hope we can finish this before the guests arrive."

"Don't fret dear," comforts Gerald.

Back in their bedroom, the twins resume their conversation. "It's almost time, Daniel. I can't wait to get out of this itchy suit. It's driving me crazy. I wanted to ask you, how do you feel now?"

"I'm not itchy. Never have been. Don't know why the fabric bothers you so."

"That's not what I mean. How do you feel right now?"

"Why do you care? You never have before."

"Forget it. Don't answer. I was just trying to kill time."

"Interesting choice of words there, Nigel. But as to your question, I don't know. I'm not in pain. I don't have to vomit anymore. My throat isn't sore and I don't have to sneeze. My fever seems to be gone; yes, I'm quite cool now. Maybe drained is a good way to explain how I'm feeling. Rather like I've been beaten up and now I'm healing."

Footsteps interrupt the conversation as Robert, the eldest brother, and their father, Gerald come to assist Daniel down the steps. Both Nigel and Daniel had suffered measurably with the influenza, and there was a time when it was commonly held that neither would survive. Nigel brushes off the thought much as he had brushed off his suit an hour earlier, with little notice of anything but propriety and doing what is expected.

Nigel didn't know when the photography became popular, he briefly recalled the last family portrait with his Great Aunt Violet a year earlier. That portrait graced the mantle over the fireplace in the dining room.

As the parlor maid, Gladys, dusted off the love seat, Nigel took his position next to his brother. The photographer did not ask the family to smile; that would be unthinkable under the circumstances. Humor was far from the minds of those present. The family rails around Daniel to get him positioned next to Nigel on the loveseat. His condition makes the seating awkward, but with some effort, it is accomplished. Daniel's eyes, unflinching, stare into the face of the camera, his body rigid in its pose.

But then this was to be expected, for this was a *momento mori*: a remembrance of the dead. Though both twins had suffered the fevers and chills of the influenza, only Nigel survived. This portrait of the family, sans Daniel, would be the only memento of the family as a whole.

As the camera flashed into the group's eyes, Nigel hears his brother once more.

"Remember me, Nigel. I'm waiting for you. I'll wait for as long as it takes, dear brother. And this time around, it is I who will be in control."

GRAVE MATTERS – GILES COREY HAS RISEN

"The menace of the supernatural is that it attacks where modern minds are weakest, where we have abandoned our protective armor of superstition and have no substitute defense."

Shirley Jackson

Giles Corey has been seen walking. Again. It's true. And it is decidedly not good news. Some of the most respected and reputable citizens of Salem have been witness to it. His transparent figure, crushed and broken and covered with mold, his fine vest, coat, and britches in shreds barely covering the white bones, picked clean by nature and time. Of this, there is no doubt. The mayor has seen it and so has Mrs. Smith, the President of the local school board. Even Dr. Mason, that stern no-nonsense physician whose practice is near the Hawthorne Inn, has confirmed it. It is the subject of whispered conversation in the shops on Pickering Wharf, and it frightens the residents, for they know what it means.

You might not think this is significant, but here in this town once dubbed as "Witch City, USA," it is of great concern. You see, Giles Corey has been dead and buried in the Howard Street Burying Point Cemetery since September, 1692. In this oldest cemetery in the city, he joins the remains of Justice John Hathorne, an ancestor of Nathaniel Hawthorne and one of the judges in the Witchcraft Court. And once he has been seen, it's sure that a tragedy will soon befall the town. It is a superstition that the locals – and tour guides – believe and perpetuate.

Giles Corey was an eighty-two-year-old prosperous farmer and church member, married to Martha, his third wife, who had two grown sons of her own. One of the wealthier residents of Salem Village, he was a landowner and businessman at heart. One of his greatest concerns was to leave his property to his family.

However, on occasion, Corey would sometimes act whichever way the wind seemed to blow. He was acutely aware of the laws of the times regarding involvement in the witchcraft trials. Any suspicious behavior was considered evil. Village herbalists who concocted medicines and tonics were suspect. Inquisitors wondered if the accused witches used these potions to create spells to inflict torture on others. Those who owned black cats were under watch in the event it might be the witch's familiar. After all, everyone knew that every witch had a familiar. Dressing differently also posed a warning. Bridget Bishop, the first to be hung on June 10, 1692, brazenly wore a red bodice.

When Martha Corey was accused by the young girls of Salem, the general community was at first in shock. Known for her piety and regular church attendance, she was a pillar in the village. Yet she was vociferous about her abomination for the witchcraft trials. "Witches do not exist," she persisted. "They (the girls) do not speak the truth," she maintained. This cost her dearly. As a repercussion, Martha Corey was quietly accused of witchcraft. With the contagion of paranoia, even her loyal friends remained silent on her behalf. Furthermore, the accusers made the adults believe in "spectral evidence" – ghosts or witches or devils whom they could see torturing them at the victim's command. In 1692, nineteen men and women were executed, mostly by hanging, because it was thought they were in league with the devil.

At first when she was examined by the magistrates, Giles concurred he had heard his wife mumbling to herself while doing routine chores. The judge badgered him, "Was it secret incantations to the devil?" Giles vehemently denied it, but he had earlier spoken to the fact that she was mumbling something which he could not comprehend. "Was it in fact a spell to bewitch someone?" they asked. Too late he realized his mistake, and so he remained silent.

When the wise old businessman realized the severity of punishment could be hanging, he quickly recanted his thoughts about his wife's ramblings. Compounding his concern was the fact that Salem had been operating without a charter for many months. As a result, the wealth and property of anyone accused could be confiscated if he were found guilty of Witchcraft. This could leave the heirs, namely Martha's sons, without inheritance. There was one caveat, which he was to exercise: a person could not be found guilty or innocent if he refused to enter a plea. This could protect assets and family.

When Giles was charged with being a wizard – the male version of a witch – he decided to employ this defense. It came with a terrible price. The authorities exacted the "peine forte et dure," a gruesome torture. A pit was dug adjacent to the old jail and he was led there.

"Remove thy clothes," they ordered.

Corey was in shock and remained stiff and silent.

The command was repeated. "Remove thy clothing, or we shall do it for you."

Two stern men rose up behind Corey, ready to perform the task if necessary. Once the sheriff's men pushed him to the ground and began pulling off his black buckled shoes, and he became aware of their intention. "I will do it myself." The men backed off.

He removed his white stockings. When he didn't move quickly enough, they poked him with a stick. "Stop, please. I will do it."

He stood and shifted out of his long brown vest and peasant shirt. His hands began to shake uncontrollably. They allowed him time to steady himself before he removed his knee-length britches. They then led him to a pit in the ground and pushed him into it face up. A wooden door was laid across his body, and then six strong men loaded heavy boulders upon the door. As time went on, more weight was added in the hopes of making him confess or crushing him to death.

"What book did you sign? Was it the devil's?" his inquisitor's asked.

The stubborn landowner adamantly refused to plea. Witnesses described how the pain crawled its way through his body and how he writhed in agony. After two days, Giles was asked three times to plead innocent or guilty to witchcraft. Each time he replied, "More weight." More and more rocks were piled on him, and Sheriff George Corwin from time to time would stand on the boulders, staring down at Corey's bulging eyes.

Documents of the time record a Robert Calef, a witness at the scene, saying that, "In the pressing, Giles Corey's tongue was pressed out of his mouth; the stony-faced Sheriff, with his cane, forced it in again."

Politics also played a role in Corey's murder. Corwin allegedly profited from Corey's death by confiscating and divvying up his property. And it was all legal at the time.

Corey died, but not before placing a curse on Salem and on Sheriff George Corwin.

"Damn you, Sheriff. I curse you and Salem!" were Corey's last words.

So shamed by his relatives' participation as the "Hanging Judge," author Nathaniel Hawthorne changed the spelling of his name to further distance himself from the disgrace. Nearly two hundred years after the event, he wrote, "At state period, the ghost of Giles Corey, the wizard, appeared on the spot where he suffered, as the precursor of some calamity that was impending over the community, which the wizard came to announce."

Time has not slaked the notion of the curse and its effects on Salem. Many today still hold the wrath of the curse. Not long after Corey's burial in September, Sheriff Corwin died of a massive heart attack at the age of thirty. Was it Corey's curse fulfilled? Ironically, Corwin, the grandson of John

Winthrop the Younger, governor of Connecticut, was not so quickly laid to rest. A Salem resident, Phillip English, who had been accused and later released during the witchcraft trials, had his property seized at the time by Corwin. When he was freed and learned of Corwin's death, he put a lien on Corwin's corpse, delaying its burial until he was reimbursed for the property he lost to the sheriff.

Former High Sheriff of Essex County, Robert Ellis Cahill, also a historian, discovered that this part of Corey's curse came to pass. Each and every Sheriff down from George Corwin in 1692 who headquartered at the Salem Jail overlooking the place where Corey was killed has died in office or has been forced out of his post as a result of a heart attack or blood ailment. There have been tales of the sheriffs waking at home from their beds to a strange presence in the room and feeling a crushing weight – perhaps like those of heavy stones – bearing upon their chests. The pain is gone once the apparition vanishes.

Cahill, however, took the cue after his heart attack, and retired from office. In addition, he believes the curse may be broken, since the sheriff's office was moved from Salem to the new prison in Middleton in 1991. Since the move, no sheriffs have been diagnosed with any heart conditions or blood disorders.

Regarding the second half of the curse, through the centuries Corey's ghost has also been reported to be seen rising from his grave the night before a great tragedy. Tour directors of the site recount incidents that have been recorded and supported by at least three people who have witnessed spirit activity there. Some feel ill or discomfort and ask the tour operator to quickly move on. Speculation is that it is because of the proximity to the old jail where the accused victims were held.

Corey seems to have exacted his revenge on at least a few occasions. Locals claim that twenty-four hours before a great disaster, reputable people report seeing his spirit floating in and out of its tombstone. This happened for the first time in the 1880s when a hurricane swept the city. Notable was the observation of his apparition before the Great Salem Fire of 1914. The fire, which began at Gallows' Hill, spread quickly down and across Boston Street. The police department sent out calls to twenty-one cities for assistance. One industrial department, the Fore River Shipyard, also assisted. Over ninety policemen from out of town came to help. The *Salem Evening News*, (Friday, July 26, 1914, page 11), has a complete list of all responding departments and where and how they worked to fight the fire.

The fire burned 253 acres and 1,376 buildings. The entire loss was estimated at $15 million; insurance policies paid $11.744 million. Some 20,000 people lost their homes, 10,000 their jobs, and a few their lives. Yet the historic district incurred no damage. Perhaps the spirits wanted to eternally preserve the site of their infamous endings.

The great fire was only the beginning. Back in 1999, another guided tour of the cemetery, forty-four people witnessed spirit activity and came running to report it at the tour guide's office. Many witnesses can testify to the genuine terror these people described. A week later, a student at Salem High School committed suicide.

In 1702, the General Court of Massachusetts overturned the convictions of 1692 for witchcraft, and in 1711 granted compensation to the relatives of the victims. Finally, in 1992 a memorial was erected so those who were wrongly executed in Salem. Can the loss of honor and dignity ever really be forgiven? Some think not so easily. Especially now that the spirit of Giles Corey has been seen again. It is not a good sign.

MIDNIGHT BAPTISM AT PONTE MIZARELA

"Nothing in all the world is so nonsensical and contradictory, save mortals, that is, who live in the grip of the superstitions of the past."

Anne Rice, *The Vampire Lestat.*

It is nearly midnight near the village of Sidros in the Bragga district of northwestern Portugal. Two young couples led by an older man make their way toward a medieval bridge where they hope to experience a miracle. Observed by a bright Hunter's Moon, two women - each heavy with child - come to ensure a safe delivery of their babies. When exclusive medical care is unavailable, often people will rely on their beliefs and superstitions, especially since they have witnessed the results for decades. Such is the way in this rural parish.

The Portuguese are a deeply superstitious people. Considering their formal Catholicism is mixed with pre-Christian practices and beliefs their offerings to saints – intended to promote healing – it is not so surprising. In many rural churches, one will find gifts suspended from strings upon the altar. Images on these offerings depict whatever is to be (or has been) healed. These include hands, heads, breasts, babies, and animals.

Sometimes, when these gifts do not bring desired results, the people take more drastic measures. Often, like this evening, it is a pilgrimage to the Ponte Mizerela. The slippery slopes and precarious rocks that lead to the infamous bridge are not easily negotiable and the women, Maria and Anna, are apprehensive about crossing over the daringly suspended raging waters of the noisy Rabagao that flows in a canyon before it meets the Cavado; but the women and their husbands are resolved in observing the superstition. So, they go on tempting their fate against the waters of the swollen river that crash down into a sinister whirlpool of death for those who slip. The bridge is well-known to locals. It is said to have been built by the Devil in a moment of ingenuity, yet the physically and emotionally harrowing journey also holds out hope and life.

The two women are now standing on the bridge. They are here because they have both lost their unborn children in the past. One has produced a stillborn child, the other has had three miscarriages. The father of the first woman and his friend are armed with sticks as they stand guard at the ends of the bridge, warding off cats and dogs which it is feared may actually be the devil's familiars in the form of old witches or grotesque demons. Perhaps, they think, it may even be the Devil himself.

Yet these two couples are willing to do battle with Satan if it means they can bear a healthy child. Rich in spirit from their faith in God, they believe in His protection. They are acutely aware of the risk of evil interference, but when the desire and need is so strong and pure in soul, these women often accept the risk.

The mission bells toll the midnight hour. Their persistent clanging from afar adds an eerie dimension to the already surreal atmosphere. It is the padre's cue to begin the rite. He extracts a vial from his cassock. Nodding to the woman, he watches as she lifts the front of her blouse to expose her naked stomach. From the vial, he pours water over the first expectant mother's belly as he baptizes the first expectant mother's child in utero.

"I baptize you, creature of God, by the power of God and the Virgin Mary." He then sets the conditions for a live, healthy child. "It is the custom that if you are a boy you will be named Gervaz; if you are a girl you will be Senhorinha. In the name of the Father, the Son and the Holy Ghost ..."

The night is still now, save for the roar of the flowing waters, which have receded into the background in light of the dire situation. The final "Amen" is not uttered by the padre. The superstition is explicit in holding this back until the child is born and can be baptized properly and completely by the priest in church. Thus, the healing powers of this midnight baptism are extended to cover only this dangerous period of possible miscarriage.

Ana smoothes down her blouse, turns, and retreats to the edge of the bridge into the waiting arms of her husband. Maria moves forward and the ritual is performed again. The group moves quickly across the bridge to safety and home.

Back at Maria's house, a great aunt from another province is visiting and wants to know about their journey. "How did this practice come to be?" she asks. "How often is it done? How safe is it?"

The padre, who has agreed to a short stop at the home, explains. After a sip of the local white wine he begins, "So many questions, my dear lady. There is a long story that must be told in order to answer your concerns. There once lived a fearsome bandit who was hiding in the remote mountains from the arm of justice. An unknown person – most likely an enemy – gave away his hiding place. He was surrounded and lost, so he attempted to flee over the Rabagao. It was winter time and the night was pitch. There was neither moon nor stars for guidance. The wind blew savagely in the middle of what would become a terrible storm. The rocks were icy and very dangerous. I know you think they were perilous this evening, but in the midst of the winter, the risk intensifies.

"The waters of the swollen river descended down the canyon into a sinister whirlpool of darkness and death. The bandit, who had lived a life of crime and deceit, had lost faith in God. He knew to beseech him now would be futile. He had no concept of forgiveness and redemption, and so turned to the dark side calling upon the Devil, invoking him at the witching hour of midnight.

"'I call upon the dark forces for aid in my escape,' the robber screamed to the heavens.

'I will do your bidding if only you will help me avoid capture!'

"Though the atmosphere was already black with not a star for light, an even darker cloud was highlighted before him. He detected tinges of a blood-red stain amidst the enigmatic apparition that was slowly morphing. The ugly face loomed before him and he instinctively cringed. He was transfixed by the scarred face that bore huge pock marks and seeping boils, which oozed a slimy puss. The criminal shivered as the Devil's red eyes bore deep into his corruptible soul. If he had any doubts as to whose presence he had invoked, the overwhelming stench quickly confirmed his suspicions. A sickly yellowish green mist escaped from the devil's slim mouth, emitting a sulphuric stink.

"'You have beseeched my help, mortal?' the Devil bellowed in a baritone voice.

"Terrified at the vision before him, the robber managed to utter a feeble, 'yes.'

"'Speak up, man. If you have had the audacity to call upon me then, you should have the nerve to ask what it is you want. Speak!'

"'There are men chasing me. I need to find a way to escape them so they will never find me.'

"'That sounds simple enough. It can be done.'

"'Really?'"The devil howled with laughter. 'That should not surprise you. I am capable of great powers, you know. In the scheme of things, your request is a minor one. Mortals have asked much more of me. Money, women, power; but anyway, you are not like them. Now, you do know what I demand as a payment?'

"'I think I do. That is, I fear I do.' Dreading the bargain for his soul, the criminal was triggered into action by the nearing voices of the sheriff and his men about to capture him. He had been jailed previously, and swore he could never do it again. 'Yes, I make the exchange of my free will.'

"'Perfect. Now there is one more clause to this contract.'

"'Yes? Hurry, please.'

"'Do not rush me, human fool! You need have no fear, sir, I can stop time if need be. You shall not be caught by these men who are chasing you. But there is another condition to which you must agree.' The robber winced as the devil lashed out his forked tongue and smacked his festering lips. "You must walk straight ahead and never look back. Do you agree?'

"'But why?'

"The devil's clawed hand reached toward the black sky. A thunderous moan of anger erupted from his foul mouth, which was accompanied by lightning that scissored the ebony sky.

"'Do not dare question me, or I shall leave you to your own devices. And we both know how that will end. Remember, it is *you* who sought me out. Is this understood?'

"The criminal shrank in terror. He managed a feeble response. 'Yes. I shall do as you say, but how am I going to cross this chasm?' He dreaded the thought of being touched by the hideous creature.

"The criminal fancied he might be flown in the arms of Satan across the gap. He watched in horror as the devil opened his leathery black wings, quivering as the appendages crackled as they spanned across the banks of the river. Immediately, a stone bridge appeared above the swirling current. 'Go!' the Devil commanded.

"The criminal could barely swallow. He was so frightened that his legs refused to move.

He was frozen.

"'Must I run for you as well? Go, you weak fool!' the Devil's order was followed by another burst of lightning and thunder. This time, the criminal fled across the bridge, recalling the warning not to look back.

"What the criminal did not see at the time, explained the padre, is that after his passage, the entire bridge vanished. The men who had been chasing the outlaw stared in disbelief, repeatedly crossing themselves and fleeing back the way they had come. 'He is in league with the devil! Let us go!' The chase was over."

Maria interrupted the padre's story. Her face was filled with concern. "But we do not make a pact with the devil when we go to the Mistrial Bridge! Please say it isn't so!"

"No, no. Of course you do not. There is no doubt you are on the side of the Lord. Let me finish, my dear. There is more to the story. Years passed, and the criminal changed his life. He got a job and worked hard, and never committed a crime again. He wanted to repent for his sinful past. He was tormented by the certainty of his eternal damnation for having sold his soul to the Devil. He went to church and fervently prayed for an answer. He desperately wanted to join the forces of good and make peace with God.

"He did not know how he could fight the devil, but he did know he could not do so alone. So, he sought out a virtuous priest who had a parish in the lands of the Barroso. So, contrite and repentant, he confessed the sad misfortune of his evil deed. The priest, who always lived in God's grace, then decided to undertake the hard task of redeeming and rescuing this lost soul."

The padre paused here to sip once again from his wine glass. "He disguised himself as a humble farmer, and on a dark night he went down to that place where he had called upon the Devil at midnight, promising to give him his soul if he would help him get across to the other side.

"Trembling, he once again implored the lord of the darkness. 'I call upon the forces with whom I agreed to trade my soul for my freedom.' The knot that grew in his stomach reminded him of the risk he was taking in beseeching the devil.

"At first he was greeted with complete silence. It was as though his words echoed across the boulders of the dangerous land and went unheard. He repeated his plea and was rewarded with another visitation. The bridge and the devil reappeared. The penitent man was repulsed by the putrid malodor of the devil. The priest who had accompanied him, removed from under his cape a vial of holy water. Using a twig of heather, he sprinkled the holy water while reciting the ritual of exorcism. The black shape of Satan, hidden in a dense cloud of sulfur, disappeared like magic, leaving only the air filled with the smell of pitch and resin. From that moment on, says the legend, the Devil's Bridge remained forever. Instead of it being the tool of the devil, it has become a religious site for believers who come for miracles. For it is certain that God in his goodness and mercy intervened for the repentant man."

The padre ceases his tale again, stretching and inadvertently yawning. "You must excuse me. I am very tired."

"But you must finish," pleads Anna.

"Yes, yes, I will. The important lesson is that you must believe that God will help you.

Anna and Maria, your families have lived here for decades.

You are quite familiar with the fact that within the Barroso and the Upper Minho you will find many, many children named Gervaz and Senhorinha. It is not by coincidence. It was a pledge of faith to God."

With that the padre stood, made the sign of the cross over the gathering of the two families, and left.

In two months both women delivered baby boys. In the church's register the two children, both named Gervaz, are listed as members of the parish.

THE WIND SELLER

"Superstition is the weakness of the human mind; it is inherent in that mind; it has always been, and always will be."

Frederick the Great

At dusk, she stood high above the town of Stromness upon a cliff overlooking the sea along the Scottish coastline in the Orkney Islands. It was a familiar sight to the locals. According to legend, she was a fearsome sight. Her white hair sprung in sparse tufts on the top of her balding scalp while it ran in endless rivulets down her back. Her penetrating eyes were a cerulean blue that glinted when she spoke. The wrinkles and deep crevices that etched her ninety-nine-year-old face read like the lines on a map that went in every direction, seemingly without end. Her arthritic fingers, bent and crooked, were barely able to grasp the coins she earned in payment for her services. This terrifying figure was Bessie Miller, and she was one of the most famous wind sellers of the 18th century.

The village of Stromness has a brooding and melancholy air. Its entirety consists of one main street that twists and turns narrowly between the shoreline and the hillside behind. The street goes by at least five different names as it winds through the village. The winds and storms in these parts can be brutally savage. They are the most prominent facet of the weather. It is not uncommon to read records of yearly gales reading fifty-two hours straight without end, and in the winter time the ferocious wind speed can easily reach a gale force of eight with ninety-mile-per-hour winds.

On its one side, the town is intersected by streets that climb steeply up to Brinkles Brae, a 300-foot granite ridge that lies behind the town. This is where the locals have often spotted Bessie. On the seaward side, the streets make their way between close-packed buildings down to the wharves that seem to lie behind every single house. This small Scottish village was the home to only thirteen houses when, in 1670, it was selected by the Hudson's Bay Company as the first and last port of call for their ships en route to and from Canada Bay. By 1794, there were 222 houses, 130 of which boasted slate roofs, a decided indication of wealth.

Long before Bessie's day, wind selling was a profitable occupation. By the end of the 16th century, wind selling had become an international trade, and it wasn't the wind sellers or witches who had prompted the interest in channeling the elements. Superstitious boatmen had set the stage for these wind sellers. Hoping to protect themselves against psychic attack, they attached stones with holes in them to the bows of their boats. The stones were known as holy flints, and were made of the same stones used in the houses that were constructed against witchcraft.

One could accurately say that "Awful Bessie," as she was nicknamed, had tremendous marketing skills. For it was because of the harsh environment she was able to carve out a successful living. Many days and nights the winds howled and spears of lightening forked across the sky in her part of the world. This temporary feat of nature did not startle her. She practiced the old ways, and the old ways were nature's ways. If one was to work in sync with nature, one could not demonstrate any visible fear.

Descending from Brinkles Brae, she made her way slowly to the shore line. She was accustomed to the salty spray that blasted her face and made the landscape treacherous to traverse. The fierce waves did not deter her. She was in command. From the pocket of her ragged, long, brown coat she took a rag of cloth. Unwrapping it, she uncovered a black beetle. From her stooped posture she huddled further down so that she could wet the rag in the water. She then laid the beetle on a stone and knocked the rag on top, repeating the following Gaelic chant known as a *geason*.

"I knock this rag upon this stane, to raise the wind in the Devil's name. It shall not lie until I please again!"

There were many forces working in Bessie's favor. Traditions, legends, isolation, and superstitions make her vocation a viable one. For as long as could be remembered, visitors even before the Vikings had brought with them Scandinavian tales of giants, trolls, and faeries, which became an integral part of the lore. This soon evolved to the practice of the black arts on the desolated shores. Out of necessity, conjurers weaving their practical magic learned to harness nature to survive. They channeled the waves, the clouds, and especially the winds. While other women in similar situations were labeled as witches and burned at the stake, Bessie used her talents to summon huge storms, thereby ingratiating the seamen and earning money as she did so. And Bessie, despite her rapidly advancing age, thrived on the notoriety and power her position carried.

For six-pence, "Awful Bessie," as she was known, would sell a sailor the winds he needed for a successful fishing trip. This included magic howsers – large, heavy ropes – tied with three knots to bring the wind. She would stand on a high point above the bay and point her staff in the direction of the wind that was needed.

Bessie was not one to be crossed. One day, a mariner named Ian came to her, imploring her to sell good winds for his voyage from Hoy Sound to Storonway Harbor. As was the practice, he handed over a black sac filled with what Bessie assumed was her customary fee of sixpence. Instead, the mariner, who did not believe in the superstition, substituted lumps of coal instead. A shrewd woman of vast experience, Bessie noted as he handed over the payment his glance was skittish and evasive. His left eyelid began to twitch. She briefly contemplated opening the sac and calling his bluff, but she had a mischievous side to her and thought she might have some fun with this fool.

So, Bessie led him to the back shed of her home and pointed to a pile of wound rope. She instructed him to take the scarlet ropes and to use them exactly as she told him. In the event of no breeze or a slight one, he was to untie one knot. As the wind increased he could then satisfactorily sail. If this still did not do the trick he was to untie the second knot which would enhance the wind. If neither of these actions helped he was to untie the third knot, but Bessie was very wary of going the distance of this drastic action. "Use this only as the last resort," she warned.

The mariner left port in the frail morning light on a very slight wind. The next day, as he headed away from Hoy Sound, he immediately untied the first knot of the scarlet rope. Within minutes he was rewarded with a more brisk breeze that pushed the craft out to sea. By noon, the sun was bleaching the masts of his vessel with heat. The stillness of the ocean and the wind surrounded him. The tight fist of humidity and the lack of air circulation wrapped him in a cocoon of sweltering heat. The ship was stalled as if anchored.

Ian decided to open the second knot. Within the next two hours, seemingly out of nowhere, he observed the clouds beginning to shift position. At first a soft breeze swept across his sweaty face, eventually increasing in speed. The wind grew to such velocity that it rocked the vessel and blew it around Cape Wrath.

He was overjoyed, and admitted that perhaps old Bessie really did know her trade; but he wanted final proof. He came in sight of his destination and thought about trying an experiment. Rather than progressing on course which would have led him right into the harbor, he untied the third knot. Almost immediately black clouds formed above the mast. Soon, the sky was filled with lightning. Thunder boomed across the water and within minutes hurricane gales of such ferocity nearly tipped the boat over. Giant waves erupted and tossed and turned the vessel while the crew held on for dear life. The wind roared. And then, just as quickly as it had formed, the storm subsided. Calm overtook the craft. The air was soon clotted in a dense fog. The crew lost track of the time. Panic infused the sailors. When the ship finally emerged and land was sighted, Ian realized that he had returned to his point of origin. The storm – or the winds he had failed to pay for – carried him in a circle.

Bessie was at the dock waiting for him, with a look of unconcealed disdain upon her weathered face. Her chin jutted forward aggressively and she shook her bony, crooked finger as she screamed, "Ye cheated me and this is what you get. Never enter my door. As long as you live and work as a seaman, ye shall never have the grace of the wind at your back!"

A TOWN TO DIE FOR

"There is a fifth dimension, beyond that which is known to man. It is a dimension as vast as space and as timeless as infinity. It is the middle ground between light and shadow, between science and superstition." Rod Serling

Quail Hollow was a dying town. It had lost its one main industry. Many have moved away, or at least those who could afford to packed up and relocated. The abandoned houses are proof. There hasn't been a new family in the town for more than a decade. Up until very recently, neither hard cash nor humans have infused new lifeblood here. We are like a lot of other towns all over this country. The newspapers and the media don't write stories about us. We're not important in the overall scheme of life. You don't read about us, except maybe in somebody's novel of fiction. And that's okay. We take care of our own.

We have been hit hard by the rotten economy, but the hollow is not about to give up. No, it hasn't succumbed to the financial losses that have overshadowed us. We've found a solution, or at least one that suits us. That's why I sit here now. I'm waiting. It is my turn to wait, and while I bide the time I record our story. No one has asked me to do this. I just feel the need. Instinctively I know it is right. At some point in time someone – most likely an outsider – should know how we have been able to cope with the downturn of our town.

None of us are happy with the solution that has been reached. As I write this down, I want readers to know we acted out of self-preservation. I know, because I live here. I'm one of the old ones. Not that I'm that old, but I grew up here, married here, we are raising a teenage boy here. I have no intention of leaving. Most of us feel this way, and I guess that's why we all came up with the idea; the way to save Quail Hollow.

To understand the problem, you have to comprehend the environment here. We all know each other on a first name basis. We share spaghetti dinners Tuesday nights down at the church and fish fries each Friday. Everybody brings their special casseroles when a family is in mourning. We take turns volunteering at the thrift store. We swap services when we need help with plumbing, landscaping, carpentry, appliance repair, babysitting, and everything and anything else we can think of. We are neighborly, and proud of it.

Roy, my husband, is a carpenter and wood carver. He does custom-ordered furniture for a large furniture distributer. People from all over the country order his tables and dining chairs. He loves what he does. We all do.

The hollow, or holler, as we call it, is a very special place. For those of you reading this who don't know what a hollow is,

I'll explain. It's a small, shallow valley, a real low area of ground. It's beyond the woods where our men hunt quail and deer. It is a forbidden place that only long-term residents used to know about – the bog that runs through the hollow. Some say it is downright spooky. Others, who hold to the folk religion, believe it is just part of nature, like good people and bad people. It has never harmed any of the locals. If you avoid it, there's no problem. As my grandpa Ben used to say, "Who'd want to go foolin' around there anyway? Leave nature be. Just let it be."

For the most part, that's just what we did. It was never a shining star on our map. Nobody that I know ever went to picnic there, for example. And lest you think it's like some hillbilly television show, we don't make moonshine down near the hollow.

There has always been an odor of damp decay about the bog. Before its current use, it was an ugly visible slash upon the wild beauty of the hollow. Now it thrives with a specific use. It has subtly insinuated itself into the landscape with a decided aura and importance of its own.

It took many meetings for us to figure out just how we could save our town. Our Mayor, Curtis Skofield asked, "What do we have that other places don't?" We all knew it was the bog. So this town of four hundred good souls searched for answers. We wanted to earn an honest keep, but we didn't want to be some other town's garbage dump. We invited the EPA for testing and suggestions. They told us to clean it up and gave us some help. Discarded and rusty oil cans, old tires, even broken refrigerators were removed, but that still didn't answer the ultimate question: "How can we make it work for us?"

They said that wasn't their problem. We held weekly town meetings and everyone had a chance to speak. We debated the pros and cons and the potential rights and wrongs, and even Reverend Buford Simms, who couldn't wholly endorse the plan, remained silent. This was taken as a passive agreement with the plan.

So, after many more gatherings, with heavy hearts embalmed with sorrow and desperation, we decided to market our service to the outside world. We couldn't advertise our facility. We knew that. A thirty-second ad on the radio wouldn't be appropriate. So our sheriff spent a few weekends in the city, nearly fifty miles away. He connected with some of the *undesirables,* shall we say. We couldn't just go to the elected officials, nor did we seek out the help of community leaders or religious folk or social services. We are not dealing with the shop keepers who make up the Chamber of Commerce.

It was a hazardous experience to contact these people. We are not accustomed to violence. We are speaking of those individuals and groups of people who have, let's say, a more primal need: those of a dubious nature who are in the business of disposal. You see, the bog has become home to untold secrets. Secrets, that for a price, the town and its individuals is willing to keep. We look away. In this way, we stay viable. I think it was Darwin who talked about "survival of the fittest."

In the beginning, we thought of the bog as a mere depository for already dead people. It's a different kind of resting place at a relatively inexpensive price. There would be no need for a headstone or marker. The price of a minister was eliminated. No funereal flower cars were called for. No chairs for the mourners. It's quiet, relatively quick, and it's cheap. Above all, our clients do not have long to wait; the body is sucked under very quickly, and there's no need to prod and poke. There is a dignity about it all, and we provide peace of mind. We need not worry about hordes of visitors on holidays, paying guilty homage to their departed ones. We never ask any questions. After all, the old proverb says, "Speech is silver and silence is golden."

But as with many businesses, the nature of the demand transformed in time. It greatly differed from the original contract. The mayor reminded us of the practice of "supply and demand," don't you know. If we didn't adapt to the altering business proposal, another place would. We worked too hard to find our business niche and we could not afford to lose it. Our newfound financial solvency, and in some cases prosperity, could not be ignored by our refusal to change with the times. With increased business our coffers were filled – beyond our expectations – and the boys' soccer team now had a sponsor and new equipment, as just one of the many benefits. The local hospital, courtesy of one of our clients, was refurbished with a new wing. Even our take-out restaurants enjoyed sales. On occasion, our clients will spend the night at our newly refurbished inn, Shadow Lawn. The limos are cleaned at Clay's Car Wash, and the tips are incredible. Everyone appreciates a good meal and clean car after working hard. It's difficult to see a down side to our service.

Today, as I sit here with perspiration puddling beneath my armpits, I wait for them to arrive. This will be the first time we are going to allow what is going to happen. Oh, we couldn't be accused of being an accomplice. Our town attorney, Carter

Baker, assured of this. We leave when the men in the black limousines arrive, and we never watch. It's like Lot's wife who was told not to look back. We don't look back.

But we do worry about haints. *How* you die means everything. Previously, as I mentioned, the customers were already dead. But now ... The superstitious say that those who meet an unresolved death can sometimes linger on this earth. So far we've been lucky. We believe it is because the dead had tainted souls. We'll be waiting in case the dead return. We have an ample supply of holy water. We hope for the best, but are prepared for the worst. That's what Doc Sawyer says when he's treating terminally ill patients. We just don't know what will happen. Same goes here.

I see the shining black limo turn the bend and stop. The setting sun reflects onto the polished chrome, sending prisms of light flying across the land. Three men get out. There is another man who wears a tape over his mouth. His hands are shackled.

I've seen too much already. Now that we've contracted this new arrangement, we've had to adjust our services and raise our fee. You see, we've had hundreds of visitors to the bog, and we need to make room for more. We've added lime to hasten the process. It's heaped on the side of the bog. The men of the town take turns replenishing the pile. We carefully monitor the lime so that we never run out. That costs extra, which we have incorporated into the amended fee. There's been no complaint about the cost. The lime is also important for health reasons. It picks the bones pretty clean, you see. Oh, we won't pitch it. That's up to the men who purchase the service. It's a do-it-yourself facility. The waiting list has been growing now that word has gotten out that we allow this type of disposal. We're getting clients from a hundred-mile-radius now.

I know some of you who will read this, years down the road, will laugh and say this was an idea that sprouted from ignorant, foolish country bumpkins. Others may harshly judge us as wicked and lacking a conscience; but I ask you to think. We cannot afford to move. We are not quitters. Are we stupid to want to survive? What would your town do? Let me tell you, in our defense, there are other small towns struggling to survive. When you love your life, you find a way to cope with hard times. It always has been, and always will be. The Bible says, "God helps those who help themselves." The holler must go on. Besides, no one else would come to our aid. We had to fend for ourselves. We made a difficult decision, and there's no regret.

We can't quit now.

They are moving now. The three men are positioned around the captive one. That is my signal to depart. The sun is setting, and I need to get supper going. The heavy-set man in shackles stares at me. I can see his panicked eyes bulging out beneath a pair of black bushy eyebrows. I imagine his silent screams. I read his plea to me for help. I can't do that. We've all been told to remember that if they didn't meet their end here, it would just be somewhere else, and we residents do believe that this is a town worth dying for.

I turn around and walk away. I cross the small, makeshift, plank bridge that covers the nearby stream. It's a gift of nature that something so clean and beautiful is side by side with the dank bog. As I pause here, I enjoy the crystal clear water as it trickles over the rocks, giving off a bubbling, comforting sound. I smile because it soothes me. I love this holler. I give a quick glance to the remnants of an old dilapidated farmhouse, whose skeletal porch yawns lazily in the receding daylight. I drift past this image of the hollow. I pass the cows chewing their cuds in slow motion, swatting flies with their tails, peaceful and content in the pasture, unaware of the process going on so close to their bliss. The overgrown lavender swishes against my legs as I forge on. A sudden breeze, like that of a departed soul flying off to heaven, mingles the earthy smells of the land with the fragrance of the wildflowers. No longer visible to the eye, I can still smell the combined scents of the sprinkling of thistle, golden rod, blue salvia, and honeysuckle near the denser wooded area between the cattails and the reeds.

I am not in viewing distance, but I still I feel those eyes burning a hole through my back. I am plagued with guilt. Will it scar me? Probably. There is always a price to pay. We all will suffer in our own ways. It tarnishes our collective conscience, but we will pray for forgiveness.

I mustn't dally. Got to get supper on. Thinking about it won't make things different. It is what it is. We are who we are. I am who I am. I keep walking toward the main road, and I don't look back. I *won't* look back.

KILLING THEM SOFTLY

"The greatest burden in the world is superstition, not only of ceremonies in the church, but of imaginary and scarecrow sins at home."

John Milton

Sister Regina sits in her somber cell, praying the rosary. She is an austere portrait of a diminutive woman who has devoted her life to God and doing His will on earth. It is a dark day and little light squeezes its way through the small window of her modestly-appointed chamber, which is six feet by nine feet with only a bed, table, and a cross. All the sisters at the convent of Ely, a cathedral city in Cambridgeshire, fourteen miles north-east of Cambridge and eighty miles from London, share similar accommodations. The holy convent is enclosed behind high cement walls.

As she rises from her kneeling position, she unconsciously swishes her apron, which hangs loosely from both back and front, frequently causing her to stumble. Her minute frame gives her the appearance as though she is drowning in the habit. A better fit is the white cotton cap secured by a bandeau and the white wimple of starched linen that is more closely cropped to conform to her face and neck.

Though she has ended her prayers for the afternoon, she inadvertently fingered the large cross, which hung from her neck as though it were a bead on her rosary. Preying heavily on her mind is the elderly nun who has taken a turn for the worse and could very well be at death's door. Not that she isn't used to treating the sick and dying, it's just that she has of late become troubled about her inadequacy in comforting her charges in the most effective way.

She knew that she had made the right choice in her life and never once regretted her decision to marry into the Catholic Church as a bride of God. Since she arrived eight years earlier in 1888, she had been easily able to give up most everything in this life, in compliance with her vows of poverty, but there was one thing that she dearly craved: she loved to sew using beautiful fabrics.

Her daily routine began with Communion. This was followed by simple chores, meditation, and prayer. She also joined the other nuns in sewing vestments for the priests. This brought back fond memories from her past as she and her older sister, Dora, had shared a passion for sewing; but now, given her vows of poverty, she was not to have the privilege of anything equated with luxury or personal entertainment. She graciously accepted the sacrifice as a small one for God.

It was while tending to Sister Antoinette, an older nun who

had been near death for two weeks, that the serendipitous event occurred. She had witnessed several difficult deaths. There seemed no easy way to hasten a lingering end. She fervently prayed for some kind of answer or means that would aid her dying patients in the infirmary where she worked.

The elderly nun, Sister Elizabeth, was suffering. Old age and chronic asthma had taken its toll. None of the nuns were afraid to die; their apprehension was not the afterlife, but the road traveled to get there. Few in this world choose to endure physical agony. Each breath was a struggle. Sister Regina had witnessed tears running down her patient's face as she gasped for air. The elderly nun had not yet reached the stage where the body gives out its final noise that signals the end of life is near. Instead of the usual rattle, the woman seemed to be choking. So, Regina went to her head and swiftly pulled the pillow out from under the sister, believing it would aid in her breathing. Sister Elizabeth was at first startled, and then she gasped, wild-eyed, before collapsing. A check of her pulse indicated that the ailing nun had successfully made the passage to eternity. This surprising event caused Sister Regina much consternation. She had unwittingly discovered a way to hasten the difficult passing of patients.

For many weeks, Sister Regina struggled with her conscience in an effort to determine if what she had done was proper. In confession with Father Hudak, she asked for understanding when it came to helping the suffering of another human on death's door. The priest's answer was typically non-committal.

"Make the person as comfortable as you can. Just remember it is in God's purview, not ours, to determine the time of one's demise."

In her cell that night, Sister Regina began to imagine a wonderful, delicate pillow. She fancied this innocuous object could actually hasten a death with dignity. Though the thought was quite by accident, and completely benign in intention, she discovered its value as she tended to the terminally ill.

As a Catholic nun, Sister Regina never thought about intentional murder. It was a mortal sin, and she was as faithful a sister as one could find. She prayed her daily rosary, walked the fourteen Stations of the Cross and went to confession daily. She was kind to the other sisters and prayed for many in the village who were needy or ill. Since the nuns had little contact with the outside world, prayer requests from the village were delivered through a revolving shelf called a "turn." It opened on one side to the front of the convent. When the shelf rotated, it brought the message inside.

During all of her prayers and intentions, it never crossed Sister Regina's mind as to who determines when an individual should die. It was purely in God's capable and holy hands. In view of an afflicted patient who is choking and gasping for air, the pleasant well-meaning sister was confused. Long before palliative care was a catchphrase amongst the medical community, she did her utmost to be kind and gentle and make her terminally ill patients at ease.

Examining her intervention with Sister Elizabeth, she questioned herself if removing the pillow was helping the sister. She finally concluded that it was, and decided there and then to do her best to comfort her patients as best she could.

With only births and good things happening in the village and all of the sisters in hearty good health, the dilemma was pushed to the back of her mind until a month later when she was called to the lobby of the convent by the Mother Superior. There, she received a package that came from her sister.

Since gifts were not permitted, she was directed back to the mother's office, where together they cut the string that held the box in place. Sister Regina removed a bolt of luxurious black damask fabric. She nearly squealed with delight, had it not been for the smirk upon Mother Superior's face. Immediately, her joy was deflated like a balloon at the country fair. She sighed deeply, acknowledging she could not keep the material.

Mother Superior was not so stern as to not perceive the disappointment in Sister Regina.

"Please sit down, Sister."

Sister Regina complied.

"You have been here long enough to know the rules. That means none of us can accept such gifts."

"Yes, I know."

"Besides, in this place what use would you possibly have for such elegant material? Surely, you and the others sisters could not use it to make new vestments for the priests. Nor would it be of any use to the sisters here. Though it might make for a beautiful throw for a chair, it really goes against our vows of simplicity."

"This is true." And then it came to her. "But I do have an idea of how we can put the material to good use and not compromise our vows of poverty."

"Oh? Do explain."

"Well, you remember that recently Sister Elizabeth passed?"

"Yes, God rest her soul."

"It was a difficult passing."

"Sometimes that is the case."

"Well, she seemed to be choking and just having a time of it, and I asked Father Hudak at confession if I should do whatever I could to alleviate her pain."

Looking concerned, Mother Superior said, "I see. What did he tell you to do?"

"He said, 'make the person as comfortable as you can.'"

Shifting in her seat with apparent anxiety, Mother Superior's tone changed to one of alarm.

"What did you do, Sister?"

"I gently removed the pillow that was supporting her neck, and she lay down and passed. I have prayed on this and I believe with all my heart that God wanted me to ease her struggle."

Sighing, Mother Superior looked somewhat relieved. "And how does this relate to keeping the bolt of material?"

Sister Regina felt as though she had swallowed a rock and could barely speak. "Since the action of removing the pillow helped ease her passing, I was thinking I could use the material to design and make a pillow to be used just by those terminally ill or dying of natural causes. It was an ever so gentle way to go."

"Hmm. I shall have to think on this. I will speak with Father Hudak and we will get back to you with our decision. Meanwhile, I'm sure you understand that the fabric will be locked in my office until we have reached an agreement about its use."

Within the week, Sister Regina, with Mother Superior's approval, began cutting the cloth to make the pillow. Though it was a small project in her qualified hands, she performed each step with slow enthusiasm to prolong the moment. From the cutting and pinning to the basting and finally sewing on the machine, she reveled in the task, alternately feeling guilty and prideful as she worked.

A month later, an accident had occurred in the village when an elderly man seemed to have suffered a stroke. The nuns took him to the infirmary, but his prognosis, said the doctor, was not promising. His left side was paralyzed and his lungs seemed to be filling with fluid. The nuns petitioned for his life and eternal salvation in their daily prayers. When he finally slipped in and out of consciousness, the doctor told the Mother Superior it was only a matter of time and that if necessary he could medicate him so his breathing would not be unnecessarily labored. When

Sister Regina learned of his condition she pled with Mother Superior to be on hand with the pillow.

"Just in case he needs it," she countered. "I promise not to intervene unnecessarily."

For four days the man managed to hang on. All the sisters prayed by his bedside, but all recognized his respiratory difficulties. Finally, Sister Regina had permission to alleviate the stress of his neck by gentling removing the pillow. That night, he peacefully met his maker.

On her deathbed in 1898, Sister Regina asked for the pillow and designated it to be bequeathed to her sister, Dora, since it was her kindness in the form of the gift of the material which made the pillow possible. Upon her passing this was done, and Dora took the pillow home. Her husband, Ian, who deemed the whole idea as ridiculous scoffed at the notion that a pillow would grant one a peaceful transition to the next world and ordered his wife to shove it in a drawer, if in fact she must keep it at all.

The best of intentions sometimes go astray when such a potential weapon falls into the wrong hands. What was designed to ease the suffering and inevitable passage from life to the world beyond became the means of cold-blooded murder.

For more than a year the pillow remained in a chest at the foot of the couples' bed. It was then that Ian's elderly mother came to live with them. For six months she complained and whined about everything. She seriously tried the couple's patience. Ian always knew his mother was not a nice lady. She had been demanding and controlling her entire life. He'd always attributed his father's early demise as a direct result of his mother's domineering behavior towards him. As an only child, she had become his burden. She seemed in good health until she went for a walk and got caught in the rain. Not that Ian felt she should have not anticipated this. After all, this was England. Just how did she think it was so green if not for the rain? She was not prepared; no umbrella, not even a scarf.

It was this action that resulted in her catching a cold, which in turn led to pneumonia. She was bedridden for two weeks. She wheezed and strained to breathe. Fits of coughing treated with steam vapors and tonics did little to alleviate the condition which manifested itself in her chest.

The doctor made regular visits, and most recently explained to Ian and Dora, "My children, I think you'd best prepare yourselves for your mother's oncoming death. Make her as comfortable as possible, prop her up with pillows, which may soothe her breathing. I see little hope for her now. If she makes it through the spring of '02, I shall be surprised. Through my stethoscope, I can hear the buildup of fluid in her lungs."

The month of May arrived, and the old woman continued to hang onto life. Her tenacity soon irritated Ian. She was nearly ninety, and he had waited a long time, as the only son, to inherit her small but desirable cottage. He wasn't getting any younger himself. In frustration at her inability to either get well or move on, he called on Dora to use Sister Regina's black pillow. At first, Dora refused. Eventually, she gave in, but only if her husband would perform the act of extracting the pillow out from under his mother when the time came.

He blustered over this, but finally agreed. Then, to justify his decision he added, "It is God's will, you know." It did little to reassure his wife. With a gentleness no one had witnessed before, the husband strode to the bedside of his ailing mother. With a quick tug, he removed the pillow and watched as the old woman's eyes bulged in shock and she fell back against the mattress. This was followed by an extreme fit of coughing, but she did not die!

All night, long after his wife retired, he watched his mother. Her former erratic breathing had stabilized. It seemed she was recuperating. This was not what the doctor had told him and he was angered by this positive turn of events. When the dawn came, she was still breathing, though asleep. For three more days and nights he monitored her progress. She was improving, of that he had no doubt. What went through his mind on replay was her constant commandeering of their household. *Do this. Do that. Get me water. Fluff my pillows. I'm hungry. The soup is no good. It has no flavor. Fix me something else.* No rest or peace for him and his wife.

He wondered, when would it end? *Don't I deserve to be happy*? he thought. Tired and depressed, he decided to use the pillow for what he thought should have been its real purpose. He moved it from the side of the bed, where it rested, and placed it over her face. Having been in bed for so long, his mother's strength had ebbed and she had little fight in her. Her hands thrashed for a short while, and she managed to scratch his forearm, but her struggle was futile. After several moments, he withdrew the pillow and his mother stopped moving. To be certain of her death, he withdrew a hand mirror from the top drawer of the bureau and saw there was no moisture deposited from her breath. Finally, she was dead.

When the doctor came to sign the death certificate, he noticed a small black fragment sticking out of the woman's left nostril. Using a tweezers, he carefully withdrew a tiny shred of black fabric. The doctor and the entire county knew of the history of the black pillow, and this fragment surely was what he had just found. The doctor, saying nothing, went to the police and Ian was arrested. The pillow was lost and never used again.

NO STRINGS ATTACHED

"Men are probably nearer the central truth in their superstitions than in their science."

Henry David Thoreau

When the old puppeteer turned off the lights after the evening's last performance, the real show began. In the medieval town of Prague, home to this marionette show, history and secrets abound; and even the one who pulls the strings may be in the dark when it comes to magic and superstition.

In this land of sumptuous Art Deco facades and Bohemian ways, the wooden and plaster marionettes have entertained audiences since the 17th century, when traveling puppet troupes toured the rural marketplaces. It is an ingrained part of the culture. Considering the history of the name of the town's legendary etymology, *Praha,* is related to the Czech word *prah* which translates as "threshold" and is directly connected to princess Libuse prophetess and a wife of mythical founder of the Premyslid Dynasty. She is said to have ordered the city to be built so as to ford the Vltava River, providing a threshold to the castle. Yet to date there has never been any ridge in the river located beneath the castle.

Just as Londoners frequent their pubs and theater regularly, Czechs in Prague are great patrons of the arts, especially that of puppetry. It is ingrained in the lives of the residents. The figures are traditionally hand-carved from wood or made from plaster. They represent all kinds of characters from all strata of society. Devils, witches, and wizards parlay around the stages next to clowns, kings, and princesses. Then, there are Czech "celebrities" such as Speibl, Hurvínek, or the Czech literary character of Švejk. The puppets can be very tall, are elaborately dressed in period costumes set against 18th century stage sets. The grandiosity rivals human theatrical productions in many instances.

However, unlike traditional thespians, marionette characters do not rely on the oral tradition of theater. Words do not convey thought. Action does. The tales are recounted visually, making the stories relatable for adults as well as children. Seats to these performances are often booked way in advance.

While The National Marionette Theatre, a short walk from the Old Town Square, presents the finest puppet shows in Prague, this small theater, *Marionette Magic,* managed by Stash Kroppish, is also unique. For here, the marionettes truly had a life of their own. Tourists had described his shows as "wonderfully creepy."

The hour grew late, and the marionettes had been resting.

Kroppish, who was advancing in age, was tired. His exhaustion was compounded by worry over money. At first, the articulation was slight. As was fitting, the one titled, "magician" made the first move. The extremities, weighted at the wrists and ankles for control by the puppeteer, are the first to spring to life. The strings, threaded through the palm and top of the foot, began to spasmodically jerk to life and although no one was controlling the cross bar, the jaw dropped next, as though in preparation for speech, though the magician was still silent. These were more ornate marionettes, for they had strings to operate their eyes, shoulders, hips, and even backsides.

Kroppish, who was also the puppeteer, thought of them as little wooden thespians whose exaggerated antics and high-strung emotions enchanted audiences young and old alike. He had followed in the career path of his father and grandfather. He had designed them, cared for them, and performed with them. He recalled the attention to detail as he positioned the wooden dowels of their skeletal framework. He had used cotton or rags stuffed into a muslin or knit casing to give them form and contour. Ball bearings were sewn into the body cavity, arms, and legs so they wouldn't flop around, giving them structure.

His lovely wife, Katia, had made the costumes for their children. Using cotton, felt, fur, wool, and burlap, she designed the more common everyday figures, while fancy brocade and bright colors and styles depicted the higher socio-economic station of princes and royalty.

Sadly, he mused, the art would be lost, as his late wife and he had no children of their own. He was a simple man. He was not handsome – far from it. His burly chest was covered with mossy-like thick hair, which was acutely absent upon his head. Deep crevices had etched into his forehead, brought on by his continuous worry over his debt. In fact his entire features, from his bulbous nose to the burst capillaries on his cheeks, were marred with worry. It was a surprise that he ever convinced a woman to marry him.

In his lonely world, the marionettes became the children that he cared for and protected. He took his paternal duty very seriously. Fathers are often required to make sacrifices for their children. And for him, the marionettes were his children, albeit naughty, and yes, even pernicious in their behavior. For a long time he attributed these traits as mere quirks of personality, rather than facing their potential for menace. He knew the marionettes sensed their ultimate demise and they were not happy.

His troubles were many. He was balanced on a mental precipice and sensed this would be his ruin. The new landlord wanted more money and there was nowhere else for him to go. Two years ago, he had lost his apartment and lived in the rear of the shop, and now he was also in danger of losing it. He did not want to close the shop, but he was starved for alternative solutions. To date, he had given free admission to the show to his landlord and his family, but he knew this only pacified him for so long. Complimentary shows were amusing, but they did not pay bills.

To add to his stress, he knew the landlord's displeasure was nothing compared to the fact that his marionettes, his children, were angry. He did not want to incur their wrath, because the last time he did so... He closed his eyes and shuddered. He refused to recall the last shop which had ousted his little thespian troupe.

Kroppish knew he had to move on. As he pondered his dilemma, the one named Krkonos, the *Father of the Woods* with mystical god-like powers, twitched his head. Kroppish was not surprised. It had happened before that the puppets, formerly lethargically drooping from their transparent strings, now began to come to life. He did not control them now, he was not, in the language of puppetry, "instilling the butterfly," or breathing life into them. For just a moment he shivered in anticipation of what might happen next.

A knock on the back door startled him. The landlord opened the door before Kroppish had the opportunity to do so. "Eh? Kroppish? Do you have the money for me?"

Shamefacedly, Kroppish mumbled, "No."

The landlord, a recently transplanted Italian named DiNozo, was gaudily dressed and spoke floridly, gesticulating with his hands. "I thought this was the case. I cannot afford to give you free shelter any longer. Very well then, pack your things and be out by midnight."

Kroppish knew it was futile to argue anymore. There was no realistic way to stall the man. He had done so for the last six months, and his time was up. Breaking the awkward silence was the sound of something crashing to the stage floor. He whipped around to find the Magician sprawled across the floorboards.

"How did that happen?" inquired DiNozo. Before Kroppish could respond, he speculated, "Loose wire?"

"Uh, yes. Let me go fix him."

"Him? *Him*? You speak as though the marionette were real."

Thoughts flew across Kroppish's mind. Were they his own, or had their evil thoughts found their way into his mind? Was *he* now the puppet whose strings are being pulled? Would he once again do as they command? A sense of madness overtook him.

"Why don't you look for yourself, Mr. DiNozo? You've never seen them up close, and since we will be leaving this will be your last chance."

"Well, I suppose I could have a look. Always have had a certain curiosity as to how these things work."

As the two moved to the stage across the room, the puppet master noticed Kronos dangling lower than usual. He knew it was impossible, yet the puppet's brows were contracted with irritation and his mouth was set in a supercilious smirk. *But I am not controlling his facial movements,* Kroppish thought.

What happened next was swift and unexpected. Di Nozo bent over to examine the threads, and suddenly from above, Kronos wrapped the strings that supported his upper torso around the landlord's neck and pulled. Di Nozo's face turned scarlet as the taut wire cut deeply into his throat, hampering his breathing. Kroppish watched in horror. He was paralyzed to act in the man's defense. *How can I possibly choose sides?* he thought.

Soon, a thin rivulet of blood slid across the landlord's neck. He made a sickening gurgling sound as he tried to speak. His effort was futile.

The scene was surreal to Kroppish, though he had seen similar things in the past. It still terrorized him. Jarred by the reality, he cried, "Stop! Stop, my child." A ripple of unease crept through his chest. Simultaneously, a dull pain loitered behind his eyes. His thin lips compressed with certainty. He knew stopping them was hopeless.

The others, including the blond-haired, delicate and heretofore gentle princess ,joined the crude, disheveled farmer as they glided over him. The clown strutted toward him, his frozen smile turned menacingly downward. Each in turn stared down at their father, their protector, their master. They turned their attention to the dead man, and back again to Kroppish.

He could hear their accusations. *You let him do this to us. We have nowhere to go. You did not protect us.* He was painfully aware their mouths did not move, nor did any sound emit from his children. Instead, he could hear their minds. The telepathic communication was riveting. He concluded insanity had overtaken him.

He stared into the steely eyes of the magician now.

Gradually, the thin smile widened across the face of the marionette. Kroppish shivered. He detected a rippling contraction of facial muscle, an impossibility since the marionette's face lacked pliability. It was, after all, made with a porcelain face. Such material is not capable of flexibility. Yet it was happening before his own eyes. He no longer could tell what was real and what was not. Rationality eluded him. Indeed, he thought madness had visited his front door.

With one last feeble attempt at understanding, the old man weakly asked, "Why? Why?" But it was a foolish question. He knew why. They must survive. He was a sinking ship, with no hopes of safeguarding them. All of those five decades he had been their master, but now he had failed them. His children could no longer depend on him. They had nowhere to go, no one to pay the bills. They did not reciprocate the kindness he had shown them over the years. So, he acquiesced to the inevitable and closed his eyes as the serrated knife was savagely rammed into his chest. He almost welcomed the release of his cares as he felt the warmth vacating his body. His legs went numb, and soon he could not feel any sensation in his fingers.

Their task completed, the marionettes seemed to stiffen again. Slowly, they moved toward the crate on the floor. In a single file, they hopped into the crate and lay down to await their fate. When the police arrived the next morning, they found the bodies of two men.

"Must be murder/ suicide," the detective concluded.

His partner was not so quick to judge. "But how did this one manage to fall-face first onto the knife? Did he not see this attack coming at him? "

Examining the hands of Kroppish the elder detective noted, "There are no defensive wounds on the hands. That would indicate foul play. We will check for fingerprints, but likely we'll only find the prints of the two victims. Take it from me, in this area you don't question. There are strange things that go on here. Some say there is magic that overtakes what happens. When we find a plausible answer we just go with it. It makes life a lot easier."

Their conversation was interrupted by a postal delivery/pick-up man.

"Excuse me sir. Came for the package."

"Over there." The detective pointed.

"Well at least the contents appear to be stored. Shame, it's not wrapped. I guess I've got to do the final wrapping and add the address myself."

As he looked down into the crate, he saw the colorful marionettes, their strings aligned to their bodies so that they are not tangled in each other's controls. "Weird little dolls, aren't they?" he said, more to himself that the police.

"Well, best get to it." He brought more plastic stuffing for protection and covered the marionettes with another blanket of shredded paper. When he was done, he nailed the crate shut and wrote out the address on the outside. "Not used to doing all this myself, you know. It's usually ready to go, but ..."

"What is in the package, and where is it going?"

"I can reopen it if you like," the delivery man says.

"No. Just tell me what you saw."

Ignoring the detective's directive, he pried open the lid and lifted the shredded paper and bubble wrap and revealed the marionettes to the inquisitive detective.

"I don't want the law to have any questions for me. Have yourself a look."

The officer gingerly stuck his hand into the crate, searching for any possible clues within the contents of the wooden box. Satisfied there was nothing but the marionettes, he signaled for the crate to be resealed. As an afterthought he inquired, "Where are they going?"

"Some guy just made a bid on EBay for these marionettes. Personally, I find them disturbing. Look like little devils. Wouldn't want my kids playing with them. I wouldn't even let them go see a show with these monsters in it. No accounting for personal taste, I guess. People buy anything these days. I've even seen religious relics on sale."

He looked at his register for the address before taking his marker out to fill in the paperwork.

The detective needed his curiosity satisfied. "Does it say where the crate is being shipped?"

"Let's see, the list says, The Old Magic shop, New Orleans, LA, USA."

FRIENDLY FOG

"Superstition, like true love, needs time to grow and reflect upon itself."

Stephen King

Strange things can happen in the fog. The world is in a state of suspended animation, unclear of its status. Time is frozen amidst the ethereal vapor, and we tend to lose sense of ourselves and everything around us. We become one with the mist. It is, for most of us, not where we want to be. It is a metaphorical limbo, not readily accepted by a society that demands clear-cut black and white answers and a readily definable and tangible world.

Part of the problem is that the fog puts us at sea with ourselves and pries us from steering our own lives. For those struggling for that control, especially those who must steer their own fate, it is a terrifying notion to consider what happens when that domination is lost.

Fog does not have a great reputation. It has many negative associations. There have been tales of ships forever lost in the fog. Pilots have radioed for help at certain altitudes when the jet they are flying seems consumed by an inexplicable fog. Stories have evolved around specific locales like the Bermuda Triangle, where many have gone missing after going through a seemingly impenetrable fog. Books have been written and movies filmed about this enigmatic element. Land offers no safer a refuge than the air or sea when it comes to fog. People walking on the beach have been consumed by the mist, losing track of their paths.

Yet for a small group of individuals for whom daily life is too much, the fog was a comforting place to hide, and perhaps disappear. Darcy was not fond of fog, nor did she seek it out. It just found her. It began when her psychiatrist suggested long walks to help with her chronic insomnia. Anxiety had always been a childhood bedfellow. She had found no relief from warm milk, therapy sessions, reading books, or relaxation therapy. Even hypnosis had failed Darcy. Dr. Brenda Merritt, unlike previous practitioners Darcy had consulted, was not a pill-pusher as a first recourse to her problem. Instead, she favored exercise to release the endorphins that led to deeper relaxation, and consequently, sleep.

Though reluctant, Darcy felt she had nothing to lose and agreed to give the exercise program a shot. The sprawling acreage at Baxter Park sits in a peculiar plateau. Every now and then, subject to dramatic climatic changes in the weather, it serves as the perfect place where a smoky fog settles in. During such instances, the four-mile path that meanders through the park becomes another world. Darcy chose the spot for no other reason than it was close to home. It was on a Sunday evening that she had her first encounter with the mysterious fog. It surprised her, descending upon her almost like a veil. She was not afraid. Instead, it soothed her raw nerves, making her feel as though she were protected in a cocoon of peace.

She sensed that the ordinariness of everyday life did not apply in such an atmosphere. That was just fine with her, as she did not fare so well in the real world. Whether on land or at sea, people have disappeared in the fog, and that was comforting to her. Her tension and fear subsided and she was washed with contentment.

This first foray into the fog happened to be on a late and sultry summer night. The land was warm, following a heat spell. The moisture-laden air dampened her hair and her skin felt clammy. Tendrils of the vaporous mist caressed her arms. She could barely discern the gas-lit lamps that shone in various sections of the park. She did not shrink from these sensations, but instead walked deeper into the mist. It was then that she met up with what she could only later describe as a tableau of wraith-like phantoms concentrated in the air, swirling and dancing in the mist. She concluded they were shadows of former humans who were veiled in a misty glow which she found fascinating. She stood her ground. Not a muscle twitched. Her already active mind swayed as she considered the possibilities. The ethereal shapes seemed to acknowledge her, but she felt no negativity coming from them.

She was fearless, and in fact a curious undercurrent of excitement stirred in her blood and tingled along her nerves. She felt oddly at home in this surreal environment. Another couple was strolling through the fog – *her* fog – and the apparitions lost shape and disappeared. She was angry. She wanted more of this world, and these rude people who now passed her by, curtly nodding and acknowledging her presence, interrupted it.

Sleep overtook her this night, delivering her into a dream world peopled by phantom figures. She awoke in the morning more refreshed than she had been in years. Her thinking was clear and she actually felt positively wonderful. *Amazing what a good night's sleep can do,* she thought.

But Darcy's joy was soon overshadowed by a weather forecast that included bright sun, low humidity, and no rain. Not promising for a foggy night. Nevertheless, she had agreed to the exercise regimen, and that night she went for her traditional walk. The exercise may have helped her physical body, but certainly not her spirits. She resolved to go home and make a list of questions she might try to ask some of the apparitions in anticipation of her next encounter. She wasn't sure why, but somehow she knew they would communicate with her. Because of their sudden departure at the sight of the other couple, she was confident they were selective as to whom they might be willing to be with. She would have to make the questions short and few, in case they were again interrupted. She longed to know how they came about such a sense of peace. She wanted it for herself.

Two weeks passed, and her part of the world was entering into a muggy, rainy, Indian summer. She felt as if she were going insane. As the rain dissolved, a mist formed near the park. She drove there and began her walk. Almost immediately, her surrender of fear when she saw them alerted her to an extrasensory feeling of something nearby. From this montage of fog, she perceived the torso of a female phantom swirling in the distance, making an obvious path towards her. She watched, intrigued as it drew closer, slowly morphing into a distinct head and shoulders. It was an incongruent contrast of a sharp, distinctly white face floating atop the even paler smoky white shoulders. A green necklace enhanced the décolletage area, making the white even whiter. Darcy observed two black slits where eyes would ordinarily be located. The mouth, also black in appearance, seemed to be in a perpetual "O" -shaped formation.

The roar of a jet plane overhead disturbed Darcy's concentration on the scene in which she was immersed. She cursed the intrusion. The vision before her vanished. She was furious. She crept through the thickening mist, locating a bench, and sat there waiting. Devoid of a watch, she sat back calmly and took deep breaths. Time did not matter here, she realized. Her patience was rewarded with another visitor. This ghost-like creature was decidedly male. He had black hair and the same black slits for eyes. His red mouth, however, was cast in a smile and the smile, she instinctively knew, was just for her. He wore a dark-colored coat with a dark shirt, but when she glanced downward, she saw no legs or feet. He was gliding, not walking. He came closer until she could, had he had corporeal substance, have been able to touch him. She reached out, but he retreated as though warning her it was not permitted or not possible. Finally, she could hear him speak, though he spoke not a word. Telepathically, he asked her if she was lonely and sad. She admitted that was the case.

"What is your name?" he asked.

"Darcy. What is yours?"

"That is a lovely name. I am called Quentin."

"That's a wonderfully romantic name," she said as she blushed. She was glad the cover of the fog hid her embarrassment. "I have so many questions for you," she blurted. She wrung her hands and her voice, she knew, grew high pitched; a telltale sign of her nervousness.

"I rather suspect that you do. Please continue."

The questions rushed out like an uncontrollable running stream, and her thoughts became jumbled and excited.

"Where exactly are you? Where is the fog? Where do you go when you disappear? Who is here with you? Why are you here? What time do you come from? Can anyone join you or do you have to, you know, die first? I mean, are you a ghost?"

His laugh was rich and deep, his speech mellifluous and decidedly British. "Slow down, Darcy.

I will try to answer all of your questions, but we don't have a lot of time. There are others, such as yourself, who walk here as you do. They, however, are undecided and I'm gathering that you are more interested, shall we say."

He smiled again. "I am not here alone. There are others from all places and times. We speak all languages through our minds. Because this is so, we can communicate with everyone. The late Victorian era was my time. We are always here, it's just that we cannot always be seen. The fog is the portal that permits our viewing on this earthly plane. And even then, it is only certain people of a very specific temperament and proclivity who can see us. I am here – we are all here – because we never found the peace and dignity we required in life. You see, life was so very difficult for us. This was the only home that offered us some semblance of serenity. Here we are content. We are with others who are like us. We are united in focus, and yes, we are spirits of our former selves; though I'm not sure we are officially ghosts, since we do not haunt or frighten the living."

He paused now, waiting for her to ask more questions. When she remained silent, he continued. "We do not invite persons to join us; their desire, should it be strong enough and so inclined, is the only admission to our plane of reality. We do not recruit, but our vibrations are such that those like you who are in constant emotional and psychological trauma, are attracted to us. From what you have said, you certainly would fit with our group. But, Darcy, dear heart, this is not a decision to be made on a whim or flight of fancy. It is not one you should make because you are merely having a bad day or a bad week or a bad month. You must be truly willing to abandon the life you know and the corporeal body which you now inhabit. There is no turning back. I would caution you to think this through very carefully. Joining us cannot be your escape. It has to be your choice; your select destination."

"Yes, I see that."

"Do you think you would be happy here?

"Actually, I think I do. This is the only place where I am free. I can take a deep breath here. I don't feel the pressure or judgment here. But I will think on it quite seriously. Only one more question;

How will I... You know."

"Cross over? Die?"

"Yes. "

"We will help. If you choose this path, and remember there is no going back, come to the park on the next fog. You will go to the first bench and I will find you. Until then, goodbye, dear Darcy." He turned back to look at her. "You do not have to decide immediately. You may come back and we can meet the same as now."

"But these meetings will be brief. And there can be no contact."

"That is correct. Until next time, goodbye."

It was a full month since Darcy's conversation with Quentin. During that time she exercised and seemed quite content with her decision. She gave away most of her treasured items and cleaned out her apartment, save for the mattress on her bed. Her clothes and shoes were folded into bags specifically designated to donate to charity. Similarly, her computer and wide screen television were also tagged "For charity."

She continued her sessions with Dr. Merritt, who deemed she was improving. Darcy agreed, but never revealed her secret as to the source of her new-found contentment. In the eyes of the world, she carried on her life as usual. She exhibited no unusual traits of her new philosophy and plans. She had lunch with some old friends. She paid her bills, though many were not due for weeks. Doctor's appointments were cancelled as well. Then, in early October, the fog settled in. She removed the pants suit she had decided to wear, washed her hair, and put on her favorite necklace and earrings. After making a trip to the car wash, she drove to the park and hid the car key under the floor mat.

She stood for a few minutes, looking back at the car and its connection to the world she was leaving behind of her own free will. She was ready to cut the umbilical cord to her life in the here and now with no regrets, and then she moved on. She silently prayed that Quentin would meet her at the bench as he had promised. She didn't have long to wait. He was there.

The mist enveloped them and she shivered at what was to follow.

"I'm afraid, Quentin."

"Dear heart, I would expect you would be. You are dealing with something unknown to you. Are you sure you want to do this? It's perfectly understandable if you want to change your mind. You can delay your decision. Perhaps you need more time to think this through before you act. There can be no turning back, I remind you."

She swallowed and took a deep breath before answering. "No, I want to do this now. There is nothing here on this earth for me. I've straightened out all of my affairs. I owe no one anything. I want to be with you. And the others."

"Fine. You know we welcome you with open arms as long as it is *your* decision. We do not want to influence you in any way. Now if you do as I say, it will not be difficult, and it will not take very long. "

"Will it hurt?"

"No. Nothing like the hurt and sadness you have endured all these years. Sit down and close your eyes and completely let go. Think only of the gentle mist caressing your skin, massaging your weary brain, taking away all of your pain and your fears. In a while, it will be done."

Time lost all meaning and she drifted peacefully, knowing she was not alone. She felt no unease as her mind wandered and let go of all of her fears. The sense of anticipatory anxiety that had so frequently plagued her days had disappeared. The churning that often wracked her stomach with nausea was absent. The heart palpitations prompted by fear had similarly vanished. No other treatment, medication, or therapy had been able to lead her to this state of mind. She focused on serenity and peace, and of course on being with Quentin.

In the morning the local police who patrolled the park found Darcy's abandoned car. The keys were hidden beneath the floor mat on the driver's side. The registration and insurance card were located in the glove compartment, which gave them the clue as to the identity of the owner. Searching the park they found her body, slumped over on a park bench. The officer checked, but found no pulse.

"Strangest thing," radioed the officer. "No indications of foul play. No cuts or bruising. Her head isn't bashed in. No gunshot wounds. No marks of strangulation or suffocation. I've never seen anything like it. I mean, I'm not the medical examiner, but she's relatively young, yet she's stone cold dead."

"I'll dispatch the ME."

"Oh, and you know what's really odd?"

"What's that Murphy?"

"She's got the biggest smile on her face!"

IT'S A SHORE THING

"Man's mind is like a store of idolatry and superstition; so much so that if a man believes his own mind it is certain that he will forsake God and forge some idol in his own brain." John Calvin

Creepy old houses have become a vested part of the landscape in many towns. Just ask any teenager, and he is quick to point out such a "freaky" place, and just ask any of the aging members of the town's historical society and you will easily get another quick response replete with the names and stories of the long –gone tenants.

As such, these dwellings, seemingly imbued with sinister tales, are the target for the superstitious residents of the town. The most frightening, of course, are those which sit abandoned for they, quite naturally, conjure images of the supernatural, including ghostly inhabitants. These structures are complete with spooky accoutrements, including banging shutters, broken windows, spiked black fences, peeling paint, and/or crumbling masonry. A closer examination may also turn up hidden and unmarked graves, bats in the belfry, downed trees struck by lightning, and spookier elements. The majority of their lawns are secreted behind ramshackle fences and overgrown shrubs, their pathways to secret gardens effectively hidden from view. Everyone loves to speculate about a mystery, and so such houses become part of the "must see" sights for visitors and locals alike.

There was such a house of repute at the New Jersey seashore. In its time, it continually drew comments from all those who came upon it. Few, however, were privy to a tour of the inside of this Gothic Revival. The exception was an invitation to the annual Labor Day party.

The most recent night of Miss Genevieve's party was a soulless night. The fog crept in over the coastline and a thick mist covered everything. Wooden deck furniture was damp, beach towels never dried, and hair frizzed in rebellion, responding to the heavy moisture-laden air. The summer season was over and the bennies – those summertime-only-intruders - had gone home. Only the year-round residents who were the true culture of the shore town remained, and a few hangers-on, like Jeff. It was the final weekend to celebrate the shore as their own, and those invited to the annual party made the most of it.

Miss Genevieve's guests were an eclectic group of people. Though she was somewhere in her mid seventies, her guests were young and old and amicably mingled as one. The unifying bond was their interest in the oddities of life. Some had called the group "quirky," while others shook their heads and dismissed them as a "group of weirdoes'" or new age hippies. It was not uncommon for the women to be clad in long, flowing gowns, dripping with heavy ornamental jewelry of faceted crystals and beads. The men sported shoulder-length hair, smoked cigars, and drank heavily. Collectively, they had not aged well, as their faces in general tended to sag and their eyes shone out of heavily-hooded eyelids. They too displayed symbolic necklaces that ranged from third eye pendants to Egyptian ankhs or Celtic crosses. Ear piercings also accented their balding manes.

Of course, the main guest was the seashore itself. The amniotic salinity of the ocean and the liquid murmur of the tide evoked a primeval sensation. During the day the sun bleached the sand, sending millions of facets of light like sparkling diamonds across the beach. At night, crabs scuttled through the gritty, crusty, sand of low tide, while terns swooped low, hovering over each unfurling wave.

The Jersey shore holds its own mysteries, like Miss Genevieve's house, which was situated on the boardwalk in this seaside town, an anomaly amongst the newer, modern designed homes. Ancient-looking pewter-dusted gargoyles perched coyly upon the sharp angles of the clapboard-gabled house. Blasted by decades of saltwater, the shingles have turned to a dark brown.

Viewed from the sand-sprayed boardwalk, anemic shafts of light crept through the shuttered windows on the third floor. Like protectors of a castle, sculptured bats and imps of all shapes and sizes roosted from every gable and every eave of the structure.

The party had started and the guests were slowly filing into the front yard, where they join the diverse mix of life-sized statues of animals and supernatural creatures. The figures always stopped the bennies in their tracks. The house was an unofficial tourist spot due to its quirkiness, but the party goers were familiar friends to these gargantuan forms that made the dunes their home. With the passing of each summer, Miss Genevieve added one piece to her garden collection. The unveiling was part of the excitement and suspense of the evening.

The animals ranged from the mild to the wild. From behind the scruffy grass that sprouts from the sand prowled a life-like black panther. A Holstein brazenly sat near the walkway to the door. A seven-foot Celtic cross from Ireland added medieval mysticism to the garden. Between reeds, stiff and unyielding to the increasing breeze, peaked the nose of a brontosaurus. His companion on the opposite side was a five-foot velociraptor, another Jurassic-sized dinosaur statue.

Jeff, a recent college graduate, had been intrigued by the

house and Miss Genevieve. He had heard all kinds of stories about her parties and was avidly curious. He knew she was old, but her magnetic personality lured him into her confidence. Her knowledge of the occult and various forms of mysticism reached a dark side of him that was normally hidden from view. Rumors ran rampant about her midnight séances and magic spells. There was a common belief amongst the locals that she was a practicing witch, or sorceress. The gossip was intimidating, but tonight he let his inquisitiveness out of the closet. He willingly imbibed her special recipe, a drink that went to his head almost immediately. He wasn't sure if it was the alcohol or the night that was affecting and dulling his senses.

Something yawned out of the darkness. He could have sworn he heard a voice coming from one of the statues. Amidst a deranged tangle of bushes, he sensed a prickle of disquiet. Out of the corner of his eye, he saw Miss Genevieve beckoning him onto the front porch. Carrying his glass, he walked towards her.

"Jeff, I know you've expressed interest in my collection. I understand you have studied zoology. I guess you care a great deal about animals. Would you like to see where I plan my garden?"

"Sure." His head was really feeling quite heavy, and as he took his first step toward a set of stairs he almost tripped. He nearly gagged at the fusty odor within the house. A ridiculous thought cascaded through his mind. Was she taking him to some dungeon? Was he being too trusting?

"Hold the hand rail, dear."

"Yes, ma'am."

The old woman kept talking. "Are your parents supportive of your career choice?"

"No parents in the picture. I've been through the foster care system and I really don't stay in touch with any of the families."

"Hm. Do finish your punch, Jeff. After all, this is a celebration of the end of summer and the beginning of your career."

"Well, not quite yet," he noted. He took another swig. "I have yet to land a job."

"All in good time, dear. Besides, you never know what fate has in store for you. Nature sometimes makes choices for you."

The basement was dark and drab. Dozens of candles sputtered in their sconces that hung on the walls, and from candelabras that illuminated the table area. In the midst of the room sat a large vat, from which emanated a sulfurous-smelling liquid. He held his nose, while marveling at the adjacent counter which held a series of beakers, like those in a chemistry lab. He was surprised at the vials bubbling in pastel colors that reminded him of Easter egg dyes. He grew dizzy and felt off balance.

Candles flickered everywhere, making the scene surreal. Out of nowhere the other guests had gathered in a circle. Rationality rebelled as he felt himself suddenly surrounded by people from the party. They grew closer and closer until they were encircling him. He felt flushed and claustrophobic. Miss Genevieve began chanting an indecipherable language that began in a soft tone. Though he could not translate the tongue, it seemed she was asking a question and her circle of followers would accordingly reply. A dark energy filled the space.

Someone from the back of the room called for another chant. The group began to moan. From the indecipherable babble, the chant shifted to standard English as someone beseeched, "Bring him to the pot!" Lanced by fear he tried to protest, but dozens of hands were holding him down. Ridiculous thoughts flowed through his mind. He felt his senses dull, and dizziness unlike anything he had ever experienced took control of his equilibrium. To the left of the cauldron the large mold of a reptile sat on the floor. He tried to wriggle away, but was unsuccessful. Realizing it was a tug of war for his life, he mustered every muscle in his body into action and finally managed to move backwards away from the pot, all the while fighting to stand his ground against the surging mass of acolytes. It was a brief respite as he successfully stalled within two feet of the pot.

Oblivious to his plight, Miss Genevieve was pointing to each of the molds that lay along the wall. Speaking more to the group than to Jeff she evaluated her choice for just the right mold. "An alligator, I think, since he's got such beautiful white teeth," she decided. He tried to shake off the effects of the drink, but his vision was decidedly blurred.

"What are you going to do with me? You can't get away with this, you know." He knew his words were slurred.

"My dear boy, you do love animals, don't you? You want to be a zoologist. What better way to embrace your profession that to forever be cast – literally – into the form of an animal?"

Her laugh was more of a cackle, and her followers quickly joined her merriment. Amidst the glow of the luminaries it seemed to Jeff that Miss Genevieve had transformed. Her amicable seventy-year-old face was now transposed to that of a wrinkled old hag. Her once-bright eyes receded beneath the heavy folds of skin that couched her eyes. He noticed, for the first time, that one eye was a cloudy blue, while the other was a deep brown. Marionette lines prominently etched her mouth, giving her the lurid appearance of a cartoon-like character. Her associates fared no better. Their faces could once be deemed normally aged, now they seemed grotesque caricatures of their former facades. There were cheers and howls and demands to "Begin! Begin!" "Turn him! Turn him!"

"Wait! I want to leave!"

"Time for that's past, Jeff," chuckled Miss Genevieve. "That option is long past. But don't worry; soon you need not worry about anything else. You won't even feel anything."

"But they'll come looking for me."

Miss Genevieve held up her arm. A sudden rigidity tightened her face. "Stop! No more!" The crowd obeyed. The chanting ceased and a tarpaulin of silence descended en mass.

She roughly grabbed Jeff's chin in her weathered, bony little hand. As she spoke through decayed and brown-stained teeth, her spittle sprayed across his face. "Just what do you mean *they?* You told me you had no family. That you grew up in foster homes."

Just as the volatile mob yanked him closer towards the vat, a man jumped forward in his defense.

"Stop right there, Miss Genevieve. I'm with the police and you, madam, are assaulting an officer of the law."

Shock covered Miss Genevieve's face. "What? Who?"

"Me!" managed Jeff.

Quickly, four other undercover officers joined him at the vat. Fighting off the drug, Jeff jumped on the idea of escape like a raft. Handcuffing Miss Genevieve, they led her out of the musty basement into the police car waiting outside. The others were rounded up as part of the investigation.

"Man, Jeff, that was pretty close. What do you think she would have done to you?"

"God knows, but I fear no one would have ever known for sure. My guess is that they would have knocked me unconscious and then put my body into the cast and sealed me inside."

"Right. I mean after the past three summers and the missing guys, who knows what she had in mind – probably this supernatural stuff. We've got to do more investigating, but seems likely she had just what you said in mind. Then when the mold was hardened, she spray painted them and placed them outside in her front yard. Good thing the sarge had us staking out the place."

The next night brought a vicious thunderstorm, with hurricane-velocity winds and lightning. Neighbors from a mile away witnessed a slash of lightning that quickly turned the Gothic house on the boardwalk into flames. By morning, the firemen had started raking the broken statuary from the blackened ashes.

"Hey Mike, have a look here."

The fire captain strode over to the smoldering yard. "What did you find?"

"Over here by the broken statue. Not much left of it, but here look at this." Bending down, he retrieved a small white object.

"Looks like a tooth. A human tooth."

THE GHOST CLUB

"I do not ever remember to have trembled at a tale of superstition or to have feared the apparition of a spirit."

Mary Shelley

It is a well-known fact that England's Victorian era was steeped in superstition, and its inhabitants obsessed with the supernatural. Following high tea, many held weekly séances with the most prominent figures of the time in regular attendance. Everyone, it seemed, was caught up in "ghost fever." Sir Arthur Conan Doyle, creator of that most logical of English literary detectives, Sherlock Holmes, was one such proponent of summoning the dearly departed.

It should not be surprising, then, that the time being ripe for further exploration of the spiritual world should lead to the formulation of a club dedicated to communicating with the dead. And so, on November 2 1862, The Feast of All Souls, *The Ghost Club* was born in London. Founding members included Charles Dickens and selected members from Trinity College. The respected author claimed he had many experiences with ghosts from the time he was a child, and wrote about them in his short stories. This was not an academic farce, but a serious intention to investigate the paranormal by attempting to expose fraudulent mediums and psychics. The club, which still exists today, included Irish poet William Butler Yeats. Clear in its opposition to exorcism or the use of Ouija boards, members conducted hands-on-investigations of allegedly haunted abbey's, manor houses, and old mills.

With Dickens' death, the club temporarily downsized in numbers, but eventually made its return in London society. Few topics were off limits in this secret society. They discussed Egyptian magic, the gift of second sight, and spiritualism. The renowned club is believed to be the oldest paranormal society in the world.

While membership took a dive following Dickens' death, there were men who continued meeting at the club on Saturdays. Among these included Reginald Chattingham, Malcolm Chesterfield, and Mycroft Toten. The club, located near London's Marble Arch, boasts a room steeped in Victoriana. The color scheme is a soothing one, not unfamiliar with other gentlemen's clubs of the day.

Deep reds, accented by mahogany woods, gave the room its comfortable feel. It was traditionally-furnished with Edwardian pieces of the day. Throughout the lounge, individual upholstered leather chairs were suitably placed near a lamp and facing the roaring fireplace. For added convenience, a small table was situated next to the chair to support the cut-crystal glasses brimming with port or sherry. As in most men's clubs of the day, there were racks supporting the *London Times.*

There was a decided camaraderie here. Men who had served together in the war shared their interest in what lies beyond the grave. It is here that for more than a decade that the above-mentioned men, members of The Ghost Club, come to discuss the supernatural and engage in occasional investigations of local hauntings. These three chaps over the years had met with the other members of The Ghost Club to get in the trenches of ghostly matters. They have visited grand castles and walked near the marshes over the moors to explore the ruins of crumbling old prisons and decrepit buildings. Haunted gardens have been their stomping ground. Moans and mysterious wails from archaeological digs have consternated the dedicated group. They have, as the saying goes, seen it all. But tonight is different for all of them.

These faithful members have made the trek, as they have done monthly for decades. Shut safely away from the chilly winds and icy November rain, the men take their accustomed seats. Dripping deerstalkers hang from a coat rack, while a stand holds the soaking wet umbrellas. It is a good night to be inside. As is his practice, Reginald has dozed off after polishing off his glass of port. Chesterfield, glancing up from his paper, notices and calls out.

"Reggie, old boy. I say, Reggie."

Chesterfield shrugs and leaves his friend to his well-deserved nap. For any of the members who have reached the ripe age of eight decades has, in his opinion, certainly merited a nap when it suits him.

He re-lights his Meerschaum pipe and reads on, basking in the silence of the room, punctuated only by the incessant ticking of the grandfather clock and the periodic crackle from a spark flying up the chimney. This sets a rhythm by which he reads.

The club boasts a large number of rooms which includes a library, lounge, and dining area. There was a room designed for those who smoked. There were even a few bedrooms for those who did want to return home that night, or in the event inclement weather made it unwise to do so. Although few chose to stay, the group felt it important to offer the convenience as opposed to staying in a commercial hotel. And no club was complete without recreation rooms. While Chesterfield can hear the balls clicking on the slate pool table, he glances at the front door, wondering where his friend Toten could be. From the corner of his eye he observes him enter, the last to arrive. The distinguished-looking gentleman removes his gloves, hangs his coat, and quickly pulls down on his tightly-fitted vest, which if properly tailored, should have shown beneath his frock coat. He quickly joins an ongoing conversation with a small group of men. Chesterfield speculates, considering the nature of the group, that they are discussing the next case. He watches as they head for the card room to begin a short game.

Chesterfield extracts his fob and watch to consult the hour. It is nearly 10 p.m. and the butler makes his last rounds of proffering drink before the president begins the ceremony. He assesses it's time to wake his friend.

Retrieving his walking stick from its receptacle, he gently prods and pokes, but Reggie refuses to wake. He rushes across the room to consult with Toten. "Eh? What's that you say?" he responds to the whispered remark. He is caught off guard. He has been ensconced in deep discussion over the direction of the next investigation during the card game. He folds his hand in annoyance. Excusing himself, he joins Chesterfield to return to Chippenham's side, where they find he is now standing before the fireplace, seemingly basking in the warmth of the still blazing fire.

"I thought you said he was fast asleep and that you couldn't stir him."

"I did!"

Their mouths agape, the two men look at each other in awe. It is Chesterfield who recovers first.

"How are you feeling, old man?"

"Don't know. Alright, I suppose."

Exchanging quick glances, Toten inquires, "Are you hungry, Chippenham?"

"No. Not hungry."

"Understandable," comments Chesterfield.

"Care to sit?"

Chippenham's movement is stiff. "I think I'll stand."

"Whatever is most comfortable," concedes Chesterfield.

"Are you at all cold?" inquires Toten.

"Damn it man, I'm right before the fire. If I'm still cold, I would be dead!"

The two friends exchange quick glances, their faces turning a bright shade of crimson.

There is a call for silence. Toten extracts his pocket watch and fob from his coat, notes the hour has come for the beginning of the ceremonies. The President, oblivious to the earlier fireplace scene, seems eager to get home and calls the members to attention. As is the tradition since its inception, the names of members - both living and dead – are solemnly recited this November 2nd. The significance of the day does not go unnoticed. It is believed that on this night of the year, all souls who have not reached their final destination are flying through the cosmos, seeking prayerful atonement from the living so that they make the passage.

Though the list is long and it takes a while to get through, it is part of the annual ritual. Each individual, living or dead, is recognized as still being a member of this unique fraternity. In more than one instance, deceased members – aka ghosts – were believed to have made their presence felt, though there has never been anyone else to corroborate the claim than the individual who made the initial statement. Often, such suppositions were taken to be a combination of too much wine and an overactive imagination. The president concludes his speech with the club's motto: "Nasci; Laborae; Mori; Nasci. Be born, work, die, be born."

After the completion of the list, the butler interrupts with a last call for refreshments. In turn, he approaches each of the fifteen members present.

"Gentlemen may I get you anything? "

"Nothing more, for me," responds Chesterfield.

"Me either," from Toten.

The butler departs.

"Humph," remarks Chatthingham. "I've been scornfully dismissed by the butler. What is he, blind? He didn't bother with me. Passed me over like I wasn't even here. I don't know what is becoming of this club. I may just have to have a word with our president. We may be an exclusive club, but as far as I know I'm still an active member."

"Well, chap. That's just it. The butler's reaction is really quite normal, considering the circumstance. Chattingham, old man, you're not really here. You have passed on this very evening. You're dead. There are two of us who can attest to the fact; an unusual phenomenon, as you well know. You, my friend, are a ghost. And I may add, most welcome in the Ghost Club."

Chattingham wore a look of confusion. "Why, I'm standing here before you, man. Are you insane? Or perhaps this is a joke? Some joke, I say. If I were dead I wouldn't be standing here having this ridiculous conversation with you."

His two friends exchanged quick glances. Finally, Toten points to the chair where Chattingham had been parked. There sat the old gent, head back, mouth gaping open.

"Quite dead, I'm afraid," says Toten.

ANSWER THE PHONE, VIRGINIA

"The worst superstition is to consider our own tolerable."
Henry David Thoreau

"Aren't you dead yet?"

It was the same question he'd heard every day for the past three years. It was Virginia's unique and cruel way of telling him to hurry up and die. He knew she hated him that much. The way he was feeling, she would have her wish any day. He struggled for air at times, and the excruciating pain in his chest that came each evening as he sat on the rocking chair in the kitchen was a reminder that his time was getting short. The bypass surgery and aortic valve replacement were mere band-aids, he knew.

Visits to the cardiologist resulted in scathing rebukes of his poor diet, which was his only choice since she had stopped cooking for him five years before. This was why he foraged the freezer, consuming nothing but stale ice cream, which hardly helped control his blood sugar. She had never been a cook in any sense of the meaning of the word, but now she prepared nothing.

His living conditions fared no better. He came to dread each summer, because although they had installed central air conditioning in their Cape Cod home, she refused to turn it on. On particularly blistering hot evenings, she would allow him to turn it on from 5 to 8 p.m. and shut if off for the night, complaining that she was freezing cold. His way of coping was to lie by the front door, trying to extract any bit of breeze that filtered through the old screen door. Most times, however, he retreated to his rocking chair that sat in the small kitchen. It soothed him physically and emotionally, for the motion was constant and didn't wildly fluctuate like Virginia's erratic emotional swings. But even the calming affects of the rocking chair did not eradicate the intermittent pains in his chest that came each evening. It was a constant reminder that his time was getting short, and the very surprising thing that he realized was that of late he really didn't mind. His body and his mind needed to be separated from Virginia.

He couldn't help thinking, though he never verbalized it, that if he had been loved, if she had cared for and tended him the way he had for her, a positive lifestyle in other words, things would have been different. He might have had more time. At least it would be time, be it months or even days that were pleasant. His life with Virginia was anything but genial. He never could stand up to her; he pondered with regularlty if this was due to his early training in the church when he considered the

Catholic priesthood as a vocation. Peace was always his mantra.

As he struggled out of the bed, he bent over to put on his slippers. Once standing, his weakened Prostate made its presence known, and before he made it down the flight of stairs to the bathroom, his pajama pants were wet from the urine he could no longer control. *My body is shutting down. It's time. I'm so very tired of this way of life.*

As he sponge-bathed, he thought about his life with this evil woman. At first he thought she was just mentally unbalanced, but after fifty years, he knew the truth. All he had ever wanted to do was to make her happy. He never succeeded. There was never enough money, enough things, to appease her.

Nothing had ever made her happy. Even the students she taught disliked her. In fact, they plain hated her with a passion. He recalled on one occasion how she scornfully recounted the tale of one of her young seventh-grade girls who didn't know how to solve a computation on the blackboard. "You'll stay up there until you complete it," Virginia had said. And the girl did just that. How could she solve the problem if she didn't know the process? It was just one of Virginia's ways of publicly demeaning someone, and in this instance, a child. When the other teachers scolded her, she cruelly laughed. "I guess she'll pay more attention to her math, now."

Everything he did was wrong as well. When he served in the Air Force she would freak out when his leave was done. On one occasion, she threw herself in a snow bank in Colorado and rolled in it until she was nearly blue. It caused him to be AWOL, he bitterly recalled, but his days in the India China- Burma- War theater of WWII were colorful. He remembered raising tiger cubs and playing taps in the band. Through his job in the motor vehicle industry, he had earned trips to Hawaii and all over the Caribbean, where he enjoyed adventures like parachute sailing over the Gulf of Mexico.

His only regret in leaving this earth was leaving his daughter Devon and his nephew, Matthew. They were the loves of his life. And of course, Virginia hated them. His band experience in the Air Force had triggered his life-long passion for music of all kinds. To this end, he had taught himself to play the piano, the organ, and harmonica. Virginia hated it. In fact she was quite consistent and nondiscriminatory in her genres choices: she detested *all* music.

He didn't understand why Virginia couldn't stand to see him happy. She was blatantly jealous of their daughter. Once, when

Devon had visited, Virginia was so angry that she took a hammer from his tool chest and smashed the keyboards of the organ he so dearly loved. Tears filled his light blue eyes as fragments of the keys flew about the room. She destroyed one of his few joys. It was the same with the walkmans Devon had purchased for him so that he could sit on the backyard swing and listen to the baseball games. They too fell victim to Virginia's hammer.

There was never an apology for anything she did. *You deserved it*, was her callous response.

Work had always been a release, until the past few years as his body as well as his spirit, wore down. Even work was not above Virginia's scorn. There was the time when he was late and she refused to pick him up from work, and with his heart condition, he wound up walking ten miles home.

Failing health led to retirement, which led to a life of despair and depression. When work was no longer possible, he woke and would have a coffee and leave the house driving to local malls and department stores. This had become his routine as an escape from her. He would walk or sit on the benches to kill time and be away from the monster, aka, Virginia.

His excursions had to be carefully calculated. He learned that when one weekend he attended a religious retreat at a monastery. He was hoping for guidance and counseling, and of course, peace. Instead, when he returned, he found her screaming and cursing and accusing him of infidelity. At one point, she took out a large pair of pinking shears and sliced up his clothing. His new suits were shredded, as was the London Fog raincoat that he favored so well. Then she walked to the closet took out another of his walkman's and smashed it to the ground. It was the eighteenth one she had demolished.

Tonight he would call Devon to talk. Never to complain; that wasn't his nature. Besides, he loved her dearly and didn't want to add to her own personal burdens. He had made his decision to stay with her, and now he would have to see it out till the end. His end.

When the first pain struck at midnight on May 19th, he was again in his beloved rocking chair. The severe angina took his breath away for the last time, and he went unconscious. The paramedics worked for an hour to no avail.

Virginia shed not one tear at the funeral. She acted as though nothing had changed. When Devon said, "I guess you got your wish. You don't have to ask him every morning, '"aren't you dead yet?'" Virginia just smiled.

Fourteen years later, her new object of destruction is her nephew, Matthew. Following a bout of congestive heart failure, she had been ordered to move in with Devon. That was a disaster. She had resigned herself to it and had begrudgingly given – in word only - her house to her nephew, Matthew. He painted, landscaped, and cleaned out her extensive hoarding. She had no less than two hundred pairs of jeans and slacks. There was clothing that she never wore with price tags from stores that had gone out of business more than twenty years ago. There were hundreds of pairs of shoes, many without a mate, in all conditions from ratty and scuffed to shiny and new. Many had never been worn. Matthew had once read that on becoming wealthy, many formerly poor people bought and hoarded their shoes. He wondered if such was the case with his Aunt Virginia.

Costume jewelry was scattered throughout every room, some safely ensconced in fractured boxes, while other pieces were shoved randomly into plastic bags. Hundreds of earrings were clipped together and stored inside elaborately quilted pouches, whereas tarnished silver necklaces, snagged into knots, occupied random boxes of all shapes and sizes.

The kitchen pantry fared little better. Matthew found hundreds of empty plastic butter tubs hidden under her bed. There were canned vegetables in the cupboards with tops that had exploded from age. Boxes of crackers and cookies were overrun with bugs.

Within three months of his moving in, her contentious personality reared its ugly head with a vituperative outburst, "I want you out of my house. It's still my house. I don't care what your uncle said." Her eyes spit hate and blazed with annoyance. Her lips tightened in a grim line, which ever so slowly transformed into a vindictive smile of triumph.

The crisis came when she demanded him to be home by 9 p.m. He had already given up any notion of inviting friends over. There was no way he would want them witnessing what he had to endure. In addition, he dreaded what comments she might make about them to their face. Besides, she forbade him any such opportunity.

On the night he was going to visit a sick friend in the hospital, she warned, "If you aren't' back by 9 p.m. I'll let your dogs loose.". A cold shrewdness emanated from her. She knew the dogs meant the world to him, and any peril to their safety would yield her whatever she wanted.

It became too much to bear for Matthew. Sitting at a bar a

week later, he casually joined in a conversation led by the bar tender. One of the men was complaining about his kids in school. As he listened, the tale hit a familiar chord within him.

"I remember I had a witch of a teacher in junior high. Flunked me in Math and I had to repeat it. Never forgot her. I think her name was Virginia Newcomb."

Mathew nearly choked on his Jack and Coke. "Excuse me, did you say Virginia Newcomb?"

"Yep, why? Did you have her in school, too?"

"No. Worse than that. She's my aunt, and she's a real pain in the ass."

"No kidding. Listen, no offense, but ..."

"None taken. I couldn't agree with you more. She's really sticking it to me. If only my uncle was still alive."

"How good are you with technology?"

"What do you mean?"

"Well, there are ways to get back at her, you know."

"I'm listening. How?"

"Do you have any photos of your uncle? Do you have any tapes of his voice?"

"Actually I do. He used to play the organ and record it on tapes all the time. Not sure about his voice though. Maybe some words to a song."

"That's enough. Now, if you are really serious about spooking out the old witch, let me know. I do this for a living. There are ways, my friend. I know all about graphics and technology."

He took out his wallet, paid for his bar tab and pulled out a card.

"Take this. We can work something out. I'd love to help somebody who has been a victim of Newcomb. See ya."

During his lunch hour, Matthew began looking for other places to live. He wanted a backup plan in case the old bat did throw him out or harmed his dogs. He had been debating the idea that the guy in the bar had planted in his head. Finally, he decided to use his technological skills to aid him in his hideous, unbearable life. His uncle's words could be retrieved from all the tapes he had saved, and if that didn't do, he could record messages himself and slow down the speed to make it menacing, yet untraceable.

It was then the plan was hatched. His decision to take action changed his daily routines. He no longer dreaded going home at the end of the day, because he knew that once enacted, his plan would permanently change his life.

Using old photographs of his uncle, Matthew worked with his new friend to create holographic images that could be shown through the window of her room on the lower level of the house. Since the neighbor's cars were parked beneath the window, access would not be suspicious. All Matthew had to do was to ask the neighbor to "borrow" the space for a couple of nights for a week or two.

The first time they cast the image through the window onto the wall, Virginia ran from her room screaming, "Matthew, Matthew, I've just seen a ghost."

"But Aunt Virginia, there are no ghosts. It's probably just a nightmare."

"But I saw it."

"Well, you may think you saw it, but remember your doctor says your eyesight is worsening. You've even got another eye test scheduled. Perhaps it was just a shadow from the moon, or someone from next door coming out of their car. Go back to bed."

"But what if it's haunting me?"

"Ghosts only haunt those who did them wrong in their life. You've said many times that you have nothing to be guilty about."

"That's right, I don't."

"Then go back to bed."

Reluctantly, she shuffled back to her room and closed the door. He doubted that she slept, however, and this made him chuckle. In fact, when he returned to his room, he stuffed a pillow over his mouth to curb the sound of his laughter.

The holographic show continued once a week over the next three weeks. Each time, he chose a different day of the week and hour of the night. He didn't want her to be prepared, so by varying the timing of the shows she never knew if and when it would occur. "Keep her anxiety level up," his new friend suggested. And that is just what Matthew did.

A few weeks into the plan, Matthew realized that Virginia had accepted the fact that it must be a trick of her bad vision. While it was disappointing to witness her fear waning, he was also hopeful, as it was the signal to amplify the scheme. Using a sound device from the car also installed beneath her window, he could play back music that his uncle recorded on the old organ. With the aid of his friend, he was able to splice select words onto a tape that was hooked up to a telephone. He had worked diligently on an appropriate script and those words not found in the recordings he voiced himself. The speed of the sound track was then altered, so it gave an almost slurred out-of-this-world tone.

The holographic images frightened Virginia, but it was the telephone calls that shook her the most. When she answered, the voice was that of her husband's. "Virginia, why did you kill me?"

"What? Who is this?"

"You know who it is. Why did you kill me?"

"I never killed anyone. Who is this?"

The voice was heavy and almost in a monotone. Each word was exaggerated.

"It is me, Virginia. You did not kill me with a knife or a gun, but your cruelty made me give up hope, and that killed me. I could have lived longer, Virginia, but you killed me. I would have done everything I could for you, but it didn't matter to you. It is going to be very hard for you, Virginia. I will not forget you. I'm going to call you and call you and call you forever, until it's time for you to join me."

"Stop this, you crank!"

The voice, so reminiscent of her dead husband's continued.

"Remember the child who stood at the blackboard waiting for help to finish the problem? Like her, you will want help but no one will come to your aid. Goodbye for now, Virginia. I'll be talking to you again soon."

Her resolve broke down. She cried to Matthew every night, begging him to answer the phone. Since he knew exactly when the calls would come, he obliged her by answering whenever he knew they were not his uncle's messages from the afterlife.

After a month, she refused to answer the phone at all. For hours on end it would ring, and Matthew balked at responding to the call. During this time that she sat dreading the phone calls in her room, he had secretly packed his belongings and clothes and stored them into his car. He was surreptitiously glad that she was so preoccupied with the anticipation of the calls she had not noticed his efforts to move out.

By the end the next week, she had again become hysterical about answering the phone.

"You can't make me answer. I just won't do it."

He called her bluff. It was wonderful holding something over *her* head for a change.

"Have you ever thought he's calling you because of how you treated him in this life?"

"What are you talking about? He was treated jusl fine."

"Oh, really? What about waking him every morning with

'aren't you dead yet?' Do you think that shows caring?"

She was stunned. "I ..."

"It doesn't matter, Aunt Virginia, why he is calling or why you think he is calling. Do you feel guilty?"

"Certainly, not!"

"Whatever."

Their conversation was halted as the telephone rang. They looked at each other and neither moved. Matthew stood firm with his arms folded across his chest. "If you don't answer, I will leave. I need my sleep for work. I can't be kept up by phone calls all night."

"No, don't leave. I don't want to be alone. I'll answer." It was someone selling magazine subscriptions. She breathed a huge sigh of relief.

For the next three nights the phone did not ring. Both Virginia and Matthew enjoyed a deep night's rest.

The respite was short-lived. On the very next night, the phone rang. Virginia was visibly shaken.

She crawled on her knees to Matthew, beseeching him to "answer just one more time."

"Fine. Hello? Yes, this is the Newcomb residence. No, we aren't interested in having our house painted. Goodbye."

He looked with pity at his rigid, cruel aunt.

"I'm beat. I'm going to take out the dogs and then go to bed. You're on your own with the phone."

Half an hour passed and the house was silent. And then the bell tone raged once more. It rang five times before Virginia answered.

"Hello, Virginia. I've been waiting for you. It won't be long now. I know you are alone, and I'm ..."

She hung up the receiver.

The phone rang again. And again. For the next ten minutes, the ring of the phone taunted Virginia. She pulled at her hair and cried, falling to the floor. "Matthew, where are you? You stupid boy!"

When Matthew returned, the dogs were not with him. He found his aunt groveling on the floor, hysterical with fear.

"Matthew, thank God you are here. Help me!"

"Help you? Help *you?* How should I help you? Should I help you the way you helped Uncle George, by asking if he was dead yet? How about I feed you garbage, like month-old frozen ice cream instead of a balanced meal? Should I help you by forbidding visitors to the house? Or should I help you like you helped your students who couldn't solve a problem at the board? I'm going to help you Aunt Virginia. I'm going to do what I should have done a year ago. I'm leaving for good."

"But, your things? The dogs?"

"They've been packed for days now. And the dogs are waiting inside the car as well. I can't live like this, with you holding the deed to this house over my head."

"But you want me to leave you the house ..."

"It's not worth it. I need to live my life, free to be with whom I want and do what I want to do on my own time frame. I'm not a child, let alone a bad child that you have to constantly restrain and punish. I'm done."

"But what will I do about the phone calls?"

"Well, if I were you, I would be careful about sharing your fears about the caller of those phone calls with anyone else. They might think you are crazy and lock you up. It's quite possible that you've made the whole thing up to get attention. *I* never did hear the calls, only *you* have. Anyway, I need to be free, and I think you need to be free as well, Aunt Virginia. I don't care what you do with the house. Enjoy it, because now you will be on your own."

Matthew places the house key on the kitchen table and opens the back door.

The phone rings. A wild-eyed terror spreads across her face.

"Answer the phone, Virginia. Someone wants to talk with you."

THE HAUNTED STEED

"Superstition is the only religion of which base souls are capable of ."

Joseph Joubert

Have you ever loved something or someone with such passion, such fervor, that parting was completely out of the question? It might be a first love with a man or woman, or perhaps with a cherished pet from childhood.

Automobiles can stir such compulsion. In fact, when a young New Jersey teenager died before he could drive, his millionaire brother, waiting to pay homage to his younger sibling's love of the Mercedes Benz, commissioned a thirty-six-ton granite memorial sculpted to resemble a full-size 1982 Mercedes Benz 2400 Diesel limousine. The granite automobile, reported to have cost about $250k, is parked on a low pedestal behind the family mausoleum in the Rosedale and Rosehill Cemetery in Linden. Proof again that sometimes when the desire is so great, that somewhere in the afterlife, that loves lives on and on.

Letting go of a loved one has never been easy. There have been stories of survivors clipping off strands of hair, treasuring pieces of jewelry, and even collecting the remains inside a silver locket to forever wear around one's neck. Connections are difficult to break.

Such was the case in the Muller family of Ohio during the golden age of the carousel. The year was 1917, and a talented artisan was painstakingly carving a wooden steed for the Frontiertown Carousel in Cedar Point, Ohio. Daniel C. Muller slowly plied his craft, methodically shaping the meticulously detailed and lifelike characteristics from the muscled appearance in the galloping calves down to the fine lines of the windblown mane. This was no ordinary horse. The nostrils flared to indicate the fury of its pace. It was detailed in every possible way. It was an equine that he lovingly named Muller's Military steed, and this is a story about obsessive love beyond the grave.

The art of the carousel was practiced with major American companies like the Coney Island style, characterized by elaborate, and sometimes faux-jeweled saddles, and the Dentzel and Philadelphia Tobaggon Co., known for its more realistically painted saddles. Each company boasted their own unique style. The Country Fair style horses had no saddles at all. Daniel and his brother Alfred began their careers with Dentzel Co., working directly for Gustav Dentzel, a German immigrant who began creating carousels in 1870. Their signature style boasted a lavish use of menagerie animals on their carousels. In addition, their mechanisms were also considered among the very best for durability and reliability. Their realistic style remained consistent, with no noticeable variations over the years.

Talented wood carvers like Muller took advantage of various woods to sculpture the animals. Appalachian white pine, basswood, and yellow poplar were the most popular choices, and where most European carousel figures are relatively static in posture, American figures are more representative of active beasts. The hallmarks of these animals were tossed, wind-blown manes, expressive eyes, and varying stages of movement.

The two Muller brothers branched out on their own in 1903, prior to the golden age of carousels. Daniel's expertise lay in his attention to military detail, with his horses looking as powerful surging forces in accordance with military muster. Brandishing his own unique touch, he also adorned them with flowers and ribbons, but it was the sensitive and expressive eyes that captured the attention.

The carousel began, not with Daniel and Alfred, but with other craftsmen, mostly immigrants who had created the carousel starting with the center pole, which bore the entire weight of the carousel. The sweeps, or umbrella-like ribs, were suspended from the top bars with two rods extending down from each rib to support the platform. Half way down the center metal pole was a center bearing, or hub, that works from shifting from side to side, and the motor which spins the structure around had also been placed before Daniel's section was needed. Simultaneous to his carving, other woodworkers, many of whom had been skilled in the detailed wood craft of church interiors, created the designs that were etched into the panels and gingerbread fringe that capped the tent-like top made of canvas. Frequently, these panels extolled the beauty of Victorian flowers, cherubs or beautiful women.

On one day Daniel was completing a horse, carving what seemed to be random bones within the curvature of the mane. Unlike its neighbor steed, which was a standing figure with its three feet touching the floor, or the horses with two back feet resting on the platform and front feet posed, known as prancers, his pride was a jumper because all four feet were in the air and thus moved up and down. He stirred the paint, ready to color his steed an ebony black. His work was interrupted by his wife, Alice.

"Dear, you really must stop for lunch."

He sighs deeply, "I know. I know, but I am driven to finish him. There is so much more I need to complete. I should add a fleur-de-lis and jewels on the saddle and tassels."

The pale blond woman drew nearer to the steed and admired the powerful-looking horse. She yearned to touch it, but observing the wet paint, she refrained. By the look on her face, he could tell she is deeply moved by its strength and beauty, and it gives Daniel great pride and satisfaction that she reacted so well to his achievement.

"He is magnificent. Oh, Daniel, he is by far the best you've done! You must promise me that I shall be the first to ride him once he's placed on the carousel."

"Dear, you embarrass me. There are other wonderful animals here, too, don't you think?"

Her lovely porcelain face blushed as she agreed. "Oh, yes, Daniel. They are all wonderful, but..."

"But?"

"He is my favorite!"

Daniel laughed and granted her request. "Then you shall be the first one to ride him, as you wish, my love. But first there is much work to be done, dear. The extra detail is necessary for the romance side, which is seen by the onlookers."

A chill wind passed through the opened door of the building and Alice shivered. She had forgotten her shawl and felt cold. "I think I'll go back to the house now."

"Perhaps that is best. We don't want you getting sick again, dear."

"No, not again." She turned to leave, and then retraced her steps, coming up close to her young husband. "Do come to lunch. I don't like eating alone."

"I will, dear. By the way, you need to give credit to Alfred, you know. He designed the full-scale pattern which was glued to the basswood for the body parts. Using a jigsaw, he had to cut and glue all the parts together to form the carving block. He's really short-changed when the credit is given. I just get the fun part with the design and paint."

"But it takes so much time, dear. And it is you, my dearest, who give personality and life to the creature."

"You are a little biased, I think, but I know it is true. Someone once asked me how long it took to complete one horse."

"And? What did you say?"

"I estimated thirty-five hours per horse."

"Oh! My! Dear, you are far too modest, but I will tell Alfred he has also done a wonderful job. Together, you have created a creature out of nothing. It brings so much joy and happiness to me, I am sure everyone will love it; and of course, the entire carousel."

Muller got far too caught up in his painting and missed lunch not just that day, but in the weeks ahead as he primed and painted and varnished the horses. Even then, his arduous task was not complete. He still had to carve and paint the footrests for each animal.

Within the next few weeks, all of the seventy-one commissioned horses, each weighing approximately one hundred pounds, had been completed. Alice watched from a chair as each one was in turn assembled onto the carousel. A new organ was manufactured by Wurlitzer as a band organ, which was played by air pushed by a bellows through wooden pipes, stops and valves. Music is made by forcing air through perforated paper rolls, much like a player piano, and the rolls cycle from one to another. She smiled as the calliope sounded the music through its pipe organs and waited patiently for the completion of the project.

Then one day it was ready. With assistance, she was helped onto Muller's Military Steed. Her smile widened, and as the music played and she moved up and down her look became ethereal. She seemed transfixed by the experience. Denied the gift of good health, and subsequently children, she took pleasure in the magic of the carousel and her very own horse. When the music stopped she refused to alight. Daniel laughed and permitted her to ride again. As the children entered the pavilion, they all clamored for the horse she was riding. She got down off the horse and stared somberly at the anxious children.

"Why do they have to ride my horse, dear?"

"Well, Alice, it isn't exactly yours. None of them are. They are for everyone to share and enjoy."

Her face registered both shock and disappointment. She grew quiet and insisted on going to bed to rest. Her reverie was shattered. Over the next month, she spoke no more about the ride. Nor did she request to ride her steed.

The first time he heard the music at night he thought he was dreaming. When he realized she was not present by his side in bed he got up to explore. He followed the music to the carousel pavilion. Her white-collared nightdress was covered with her flimsy, fringed shawl, not nearly sufficient to insulate her from the drafty pavilion. He took a moment to assess her; he could not deny her thin, gaunt face. As she held tightly to the brass pole of the steed, he noticed the bones protruding from her wrists, so lean were her arms. His heart panged with sadness and he was reminded of a visage of an emaciated waif, or perhaps a sacred cherub and he grew alarmed. He trembled at the thought of her frailty. But how could he be angry with her? She asked for nothing.

He considered leaving her on the carousel a while longer, but the dampness worried him. He allowed her a few more minutes before striding to the ride and turning it on. *Surely one ride could not harm her,* he thought.

Once the ride had finished its rotations, he came to her in silence and lifted her off her horse and carried her back to their room. He would have to be more alert to her wanderings at night, or else accompany a more warmly dressed wife. She nestled her head beneath his chin and spoke to him so softly, her words were barely audible. "Dear, I think I should love to ride my horse into heaven, someday."

"Hm?"

"Oh, just that I love that horse so dearly. I would love to be with him always."

"Dear, you shall have a whole life time of riding the horse."

"I doubt that, dearest."

"What?"

"Nothing, dear. Just so tired."

To no one's surprise Alice contracted spring flu. As she took in her last breath, with a tremor in her voice, she murmured, "My horse, my horse, Daniel. Forever mine. I *shall* ride him into heaven." And though she fought it valiantly, like a dying star, her life winked out. Daniel was bereft and inconsolable. He moved in with his brother, but he could not work. His thoughts were always with Alice.

It was shortly after her passing later in the summer that people reported a haunting on the carousel. It began with the stories of two children who swore there was a blond-haired woman who rode the black steed. Her face, they said, "was as white as a ghost," and her eyes were rimmed red as though she had been crying for a long time. When they approached her, she did not speak. When they neared her, she vanished! Since her passing, Daniel did not live near the carousel, but the tales of its haunting traveled back to him. He visited the carousel frequently to see if it was his dear Alice who was still riding her steed after death. He did not observe her.

However, he did consult a medium. "What is a ghost?" the woman began. "It is a spirit that cannot move beyond this realm. Since not everyone can see her, I do not think she is an actual spirit apparition. That is not to say that her presence is not viable. I believe that she suffers from emotional shock and being parted from this horse that you created for her. As such, she wants to continually relive certain moments."

Noting Daniel's confusion, she explained that Alice was an example of residual energy. "Think of when a woman wears too much perfume. She leaves the room, and the scent remains. That's what is the case here. Though she has departed, her energy still remains."

"But what can I do?" Daniel beseeched. "The amusement park is upset and they keep saying that the carousel is no longer an asset to the park. If they destroy it, I don't know what will happen with Alice."

"Then have them remove it. Or at least that one horse. Let it be a memorial to both Alice and the horse."

A light began to flicker in Daniel's weary, sad eyes. The very next day, he approached the director of the park. It took several meetings, but within the next few months the management of the park decided the negative publicity was detrimental to the ride and decided to retire the black military steed. Daniel begged the owners to disassemble the horse from the carousel, and it was placed in a glass display case in the basement of the pavilion. On the day of the transfer, a child came running to find Daniel, hearing about the move.

"Mister, I thought you might like to have this." He held out his hand and in the palm was an ivory colored fringe from a woman's shawl. "I found it by the special black horse on the merry-go-round," he said. "I was going to keep it, sort of like a treasure," the young boy confessed, "but then I remembered how sad you were about your wife and how much she loved the horse and I thought you might like to have it."

"What a kind thing you've done, son."

Daniel recognized it at once as part of Alice's shawl. He found a beautiful satin pink ribbon and tied the fringe onto the horn of the saddle of her steed, and asked if he could dedicate the horse to his wife with a photograph of her atop the celebrated animal. When the management agreed, he breathed a sigh of relief. The fringed shawl was the proof he had been waiting for. Deep in his heart, he knew that Alice had rode Muller's steed right into heaven.

WEREWOLF FEVER

"Most people who offer their help do it to make themselves feel better, not us. To be honest, I don't blame them. It's superstition: If you give assistance to the family in need... if you throw salt over your shoulder... if you don't step on the cracks, then maybe you'll be immune. Maybe you'll be able to convince yourself that this could never happen to you."

Jodi Picoult, Handle With Care

He stands in all his fury and hunger in front of the child. He ignores the soreness of the mange that covers spots over his back. It is time for him to eat. The hunger ravages his stomach, and he roars in frustration. He snarls, displaying his teeth. Saliva drools from his mouth, glossing over his fangs. His hackles are raised. His posture assumes an attack position. He has cornered the girl; she has nowhere to run. There is no rush. Were he of a nature that relished the kill, he would have lingered even longer, but his quest is based purely on the need to feed before the season of cold sets in.

The child is frozen in fear. She does not move, but stares into the creature's eyes, seemingly transfixed into inaction. He misreads the fear and instead takes this as a challenge and leaps onto his prey. She feels no fear; she is numb. When he takes the first bite from her fleshy arm she mercifully passes out.

The peasants of Dole, in Franche Comte, discovered the young girl. They were repulsed by the condition in which her child's body had been mutilated, but they were not surprised. She was not the first to meet such a horrid fate. Three others, a young boy and two women, had fallen victims to the voracious carnivore. The wolves had, as of late, been attacking closer and closer to their huts. And with Michaelmas on September 29th, only days away, and the coming weather, they knew this will not be the end of the attacks. It was a significant time, as this feast which honors Saint Michael, the Archangel, falls near the autumnal equinox and ushers in the shortening of the days as well as the ending and beginning of the husbandman's year of harvest, which in turn meant the collection of crops from the reeve of the manor.

Not everyone in the small village was aware of the danger from the wolves. There were those relatively new to the area, like Gilles Garnier. He had waited a long time to settle down. He knew from others' reactions that he was not a handsome or desirable man, and appearances spoke volumes. Many described him as strange-looking, in part, he guessed, because his posture was stooped over. The most disconcerting feature, however, were the dark bushy eyebrows that knitted together above his eyes, seeming as though it were one long brow. This stood out against his extremely pale skin.

He had been a recluse for many years, even after he married his wife, Apolline. He had fathered two children. It was

1573, and they had just left their hut outside of Lyons and come to the village of Dole. In a well-hidden spot, shrouded in trees near Amanges, the family settled. Their hut was the most rudimentary, with a turf roof and mud walls that were blotched with lichen. The trampled garden was in ruins and the fence in shambles. The hut was far from any road and could only be reached by a path over moorland and through dense forest. Partly because it was so inaccessible, and also because the family was deemed strange, they had few visitors.

Gilles was good at hunting. He daily scoured the woods for game. Because the family did not socialize and he looked odd with his extremely long gray beard, he was given the name "the hermit of S. Bonnot." The other peasants sensed he was different. He seldom spoke, and when he did it was in the vernacular of his home. It was clear to all that he and his family did not fit in.

As time wore on, Gilles heard of the wolf attacks. It was September 9th, days before Michaelmas or the feast of Saint Michael celebrated widely in the 16th century. He expected the arrival of the bailiff to tally his harvest.

It was not long after that a ten -year-old girl wandered into a vineyard. She was attacked by a wolf. Those who found her had heard the baying of a wolf. Her body was dragged deep into the woods, where her clothes were torn off and she was bitten and partially devoured. The peasants found the child with her flesh raw and swarming with insects.

The peasants began to talk. "It was bad before, but it is getting worse. That hermit is always hunting. How do we know it was not him?"

All of the other men considered what was being said. Their superstitious minds began to work overtime, and it wasn't long before Gilles was a suspect in the two killings. However, there was no proof.

Throughout the village superstition reigned supreme. It was as though a fever had erupted and the sickness began to spread. From one mouth to another, the infection spread and the masses grew hostile. Their guard was on full alert.

Because of his lack of social status, Gilles was ignorant of their speculations. He kept hunting, and the peasants continued their watch. Within a week, a young boy was the victim of another wolf attack. At dusk, the villagers came upon the scene. The boy's flesh was ripped from his thighs and belly, and one leg was missing. Then, they spotted Gilles walking with his hunting sack apparently filled. His prey seemed heavy, as he dragged it along the ground. He had literally been the wrong place at the wrong time.

It wasn't a far stretch for these ignorant and uneducated peasants to jump to the conclusion that it wasn't an ordinary wolf that had been committing the murders. Drawing on their superstitions, they targeted Gilles as a loup-garrou – a werewolf.

Werewolf fever ran high. Things that could not be simply explained or understood took on supernatural elements.

"His table is always full," some said.

"Yes, we hunt the same place and often we have trouble finding game. Perhaps he has an edge on us."

The peasants went to Gilles' hut and accused him of being a werewolf. Armed with pitchforks and axes and crosses and Bibles, they confronted him.

"I think I seen him kill him with both his hands, they looked like paws, and he tore into his flesh with long teeth!"

"He feeds his wife with this meat!" another added.

The others were quick to follow with accusations. Hysteria ruled the day. More than fifty villagers claimed they had been witnesses to his savage attacks.

The peasants visited the magistrate and explained the situation. The court agreed that indeed Gilles Garnier had been under the dark spell of something wicked and not of this earth. But it wasn't enough to recognize evil. It had to be purged from the village.

The Parliament of Franche-Comte decided to make an example of him. "Our blessed St. Michael, who defeated Satan, knows his powers. If anyone dares to make a pact with the devil, there will be fatal consequences. Not just on this earth, but in the afterlife as well!"

The peasants of the neighborhood of Dole were authorized by the Court of Parliament at Dole to hunt down any other werewolves who infested the country. "According to the advertisement made to the sovereign Court of Parliament at Dole, that, in the territories of Espagny, Salvange, Courchapon, and the neighboring villages, has often been seen and met, for some time past, a werewolf, who, it is said, has already seized and carried off several little children, so that they have not been seen since, and since he has attacked and done injury in the country to some horsemen, who kept him off only with great difficulty and danger to their persons; the said Court, desiring to prevent any greater danger, has permitted, and does permit, those who are abiding or dwelling in the said places and others, notwithstanding all edicts concerning the chase, to assemble with pikes, halberds, arquebuses, and sticks, to chase and to pursue the said werewolf in every place where they may find or seize him; to tie and to kill, without incurring any pains or penalties." The document was signed on the 13th day of September, 1573.

Fear and excruciating pain can make one say and do strange things. Inhumane torture has always elicited confession, whether true or not. Not accustomed to any kind of real social interaction, Gilles panicked and caved in. When confronted by the angry peasants, he tried to explain away the coincidence of his circumstances to the violence, but no one would listen. Yet he did not confess, nor claim to change into a werewolf.

To urge a confession, the magistrate commanded he be placed in the rack. By stretching and dislocating his body, it was expected the strange hermit would talk. This was viewed as a totally legal means for justice to extract the truth. The rack consisted of a rectangular wooden frame that had a roller at each end. Garnier's feet were manacled to one roller and his wrists to the other. A handle and ratchet were attached to the top roller and were turned very gradually stepwise to increase the tension on the chains. He was tied across a board by his ankles and wrists. The rollers at each end of the board were turned, pulling his body in opposite directions. Initially his body was merely stretched, but after a short while his limbs were dislocated. Before his limbs were torn from their sockets, he told them what they wanted to hear.

"I was in the woods one day," he mumbled, "trying to shoot a deer for our meal. Out of nowhere I came upon a strange specter that resembled a man with horns." He was gasping now, but the magistrate would have none of it. "Speak up!"

He repeated his story.

"The devil!' the peasants cried out.

"Let him speak!" The audience grew silent.

"It was a dark force outside of me. He offered me an ointment and said if I rubbed it over my body I could change into a wolf. It would make me the best hunter, since the power of a wolf was such that it would help me get more food in less time. We would never go hungry!"

"Mon Dieu!" they said in unison.

The peasants were in awe of such a transformation from man to beast.

The group gathered around him and tied his wife's hands behind her back. The mob pushed, dragged, and towed them into the hut of the magistrate, where both husband and wife were placed under arrest.

The accusations continued. In another account, the indictment read against him by Henri Camus, doctor of laws and counselor of the king, asserted that Garnier had come upon a twelve year-old girl in a vineyard and killed her with his teeth and hands, tearing her apart. From the scene of the crime he had trailed her bleeding body along the ground with his teeth into the woods of La Serre, where he consumed most of her and carried the rest back to his wife. In addition, fifteen days after the festival of All Saints, in the shape of a wolf he devoured a boy of thirteen years of age, having previously torn off his leg and hid them for eating at a later date.

Appolline was called before the court to testify. She agreed that her husband had been a great hunter with the unusual ability to always bring home great quantities of meat and game. She denied knowing the source of the food, but concurred that she had eaten it. The court agreed that indeed Gilles Garnier had been under the dark spell of something supernatural, but it wasn't enough to recognize evil. It had to be purged from the village.

Normally, they would have strangled him as a mercy before burning him, since he had confessed of his own accord; but believing the crimes so heinous, the court sentenced him to burning alive.

The torch was lit on January 8, 1574, and the peasants watched as Gilles writhed in agony. His screams, some said, could be heard in the next village. The smoke from the searing flesh polluted the country air.

"Suffer as ye made others suffer!" some in the crowd yelled.

The really frightening thing was that several of those who were present swore they saw his face turn into that of a wolf.

In the ensuing weeks, the wolf attacks increased and this time the victims were adults.

Peasants were at a loss to explain how this could be, since the real werewolf, Gilles Garnier, had burnt at the stake.

Slaves to Superstition

The very word "superstition," which stems from the Latin, has two meanings: one is to "stand over something," the other is "to outlive." Superstitions continue to exist because our belief systems are so strong that we perpetuate them; often "just in case" they may come to transpire. The psychological power they hold over us is often incredible. Sometimes our beliefs are stronger than the truth.

Superstitions know no bounds when it comes to religion, class or ethnicity, and it is in itself a myth that only the common folk practice and propagate superstitions. The truth is that celebrities in all walks of life have been victim to superstitions, and it has been the case for as long as man has recorded history, and quite probably before that. Pagans and early Christians were no strangers to such belief systems, some of which we still believe today in our modern age of technology. Despite our fast-track, instant-messaging lifestyles, ancient beliefs still hold sway over our imaginations and our lives.

You'll find superstitions in politics, history, sports, literature, music, and psychology; in essence, every walk of life. The reader will find omens and superstitions in the works of Shakespeare, Mark Twain, Henry James, Edgar Allen Poe, and Shirley Jackson. Musicians hold their own belief systems when it comes to certain numbers. There are superstitions surrounding the Apollo Space Program, WWI British intelligence, and even Masonic influences in Washington, D.C. Holidays are chock full of superstitions, as are the simplest of nursery rhymes.

Superstitions can take the form of a belief in an event, a day such as a holiday, a number, or even an object. The wearing of specific colors carries a great deal of significance to some, while royalty have held superstitions regarding certain foods, such as the Ukrainian people who treasure their symbolic Pysanky eggs. Jewelry takes its own place in the world of superstitions, while talismans have long been favorites of American presidents, musicians, sports figures, and everyday people. Read on to find some interesting anecdotes about some of the believers.

Actors

Actors are traditionally a superstitious lot. Whether bit players or stars, they follow certain beliefs. For example, legendary horror actor **Boris Karloff,** who created the role of Frankenstein and went on to appear in dozens of other "monster" roles, refused to perform on a radio show on Friday the 13th.

In 1967, Laurence Olivier and **Peter Ustinov** were nominated by the Television Academy for the same Emmy award. Olivier was not able to be present, so he requested that Ustinov should accept for him if he won. Ustinov was superstitious about preparing an acceptance speech in advance for himself, but he was prepared to accept for Olivier. It was Ustinov who won the award and, stammering and changing a word or sentence here and there, he used the Olivier speech for his own acceptance.

Jessica Alba: At her baby shower, she asked all in attendance to wear a leather bracelet with prayers on it. She asked them not to remove them until after her baby was born. She believed that once the bracelet was removed it would bring bad luck to her daughter and do her harm.

Actress **Lindsey Lohan Lindsay** wears a $3000 "evil eye" necklace to bring her good luck.

Actress/model **Megan Fox** is afraid of flying. Whenever she's on a plane, she listens to Britney Spears as she believes it's "not her destiny to die listening to a Britney Spears album."

Robin Williams carries a lucky carved ivory figurine that belonged to his father.

Actress **Cameron Diaz** frequently knocks on wood and has several lucky charms, one of which is a necklace she wears to ward off the signs of aging.

Brad Pitt wears a shark tooth necklace he believes will protect him from danger.

Artists

The artistic temperament is often mercurial. Mood swings, "periods" of their lives, and their art impact their belief systems. **Pablo Picasso** was a very superstitious man. He never permitted his wife, Francoise Gilot, to lay his hat on the bed for fear that someone would die in the next year. Also, whenever she opened an umbrella in the house he insisted it meant bad luck. To reverse it, he insisted she march with her fingers crossed over her head and join him in shouting "Legarto."

Authors

Though **Mark Twain** claimed to abhor superstitions, he had a prediction. He was born on the day Haley's Comet passed and he predicted he would "go out" when the next one made its appearance seventy-six years later. He died on that exact day.

Charles Dickens was one of the most popular writers of his time, but that didn't stop him from paying heed to old wives' tales. A first edition copy of David Copperfield, due to be auctioned by Christie's in June, reveals the extent of the Victorian writer's superstitious nature. If a knife is given as a gift, the superstition goes that the relationship between giver and recipient will end soon. To avoid this, coin or another gift must be given in return.

In order to banish bad omens, the writer inscribed his own personal copy of *David Copperfield* (the novel he described as his 'favourite child') and sent it to the owner of Sheffield tool company, William Brookes and Sons after the manufacturer gave Dickens a box of cutlery.

The exchange happened after William Brookes read the novel in 1850 and noticed that the main character was ridiculed with the nickname 'Brooks of Sheffield'. When he then wrote to Dickens to express his surprise, the writer responded and called it 'one of those remarkable coincidences.'

Film Directors

Alfred Hitchcock became slightly superstitious that his films could only be successful if he was in them.

Historical Figures:

Superstitions take many forms. Placing one's fate in the hands of an object, trinket, or piece of jewelry is a common trend amongst royalty over the centuries.

Catherine de Medici was one of the most superstitious queens of her day, and even showed a natural talent for alchemy and astrology. Catherine's most famous talisman was her love talisman, made from metals melted during favorable astrological signs and then mixed with human and goat blood.

Catherine II, aka Catherine the Great of Russia believed that the consumption of chicken gizzards would bring her fertility. It seemed to have worked, as after eight years of marriage she finally gave birth to three children. (Some do, however, question their paternity!)

For hundreds of years, royalty cherished amulets and talismans as protection. **Mary Queen of Scots** possessed unicorn horns to ward off illness. Not long before her execution she had a silver skull watch made. It is opened by dropping the under jaw, which turns upon a hinge, while the watch works occupy the place of the brain.

Henry VII also possessed a serpent's tongue on a chain to protect him from sudden poisoning and illnesses.

Musicians

Wolfgang Amadeus Mozart was a very superstitious person who was afraid of the dark and supernatural beings. He had a difficult time writing his requiem mass because he feared that this mass would be honoring his own death. As a result, he procrastinated in writing it.

Country singer, Garth Brooks has carried around three lucky seeds for eighteen years after they helped him triumph at an award ceremony. He won prizes at the 1990 Association of Country Music Awards and is convinced the lucky buckeye seeds given to him by a fan are responsible for his success. He carries them everywhere.

According to the Chaldean numerology, the number twenty-seven is a spiritual number which, some believe, has the power to break one's wheel of life and death. The concept has been revisited many times considering the early death of **Jim Morrison, Janis Joplin, Brian Jones, Jimi Hendrix, Pete Ham, Kurt Cobain,** and **Amy Winehouse,** all passing at the age of twenty-seven. This has been dubbed they are members of the **Forever Twenty-Seven Club.**

Guns and Roses front man **Axel Rose** has a very bizarre superstition about the alphabet and the letter M, in particular. He never plays concerts in cities starting with M. Axel thinks this letter brings bad luck, as it is cursed.

Politicians

Former Prime Minister of India, Indira Gandhi, consulted soothsayers and astrologers.

Pakistan's president, Asif Ali Zardi slaughtered black goats every day since taking office to thwart the evil eye.

President William McKinley made a habit of wearing a red carnation in his lapel for luck. Occasionally, when he wanted to share the luck with others, he would give it away. For example, if someone asked him for a favor he couldn't grant, he would offer the carnation as a consolation prize.

Once, when two boys were visiting him in the White House, he gave one boy the carnation from his lapel, then he shrewdly took another out of a vase to put into his lapel for a while before giving that one to the other boy, so his blossom would be lucky too.

US President Franklin D. Roosevelt strongly believed that it was bad luck to light three cigarettes with one match. Roosevelt had an acute case of triskaidekaphobia, or fear of the number thirteen. He would invite his secretary to come to dinner with him if there were otherwise going to be thirteen guests present at the function. If his party was going to travel on the thirteenth of the month, he would reschedule the departure for 11:50 p.m. on the twelfth or 12:10 a.m. on the fourteenth. He avoided the date even in death, passing away in April 1945, on the afternoon of Thursday the twelfth.

In the 1880s, **The Thirteen Club** was created to debunk the superstition of thirteenth at a table being unlucky. This belief states that when thirteen people are seated together at a table, one will die within a year. They met on the thirteenth of the month for a dinner served to thirteen people at each table. By 1887, The Thirteen Club was 400-strong, over time gaining five United States Presidents as honorary members including **Chester Arthur, Grover Cleveland, Benjamin Harrison, William McKinley, and Theodore Roosevelt.**

The "thirteen at a table" superstition may take its origin from The Last Supper, wherein thirteen people dined (Jesus and his twelve disciples), and Jesus died soon after; or from the Valhalla Banquet story in Norse mythology. That story tells about twelve gods invited to a banquet. Loki, making thirteen, intrudes and Balder, the favorite of the gods, is killed.

Psychiatrists

There's no doubt that **Sigmund Freud** was a brilliant man, but even brilliant men have their idiosyncrasies. One of Freud's was an obsession with numbers. Some of this may have stemmed from his knowledge of Jewish mysticism, or it could have been from his studying under Wilhelm Fliess, the discoverer of biorhythms, who himself saw almost magical properties in the numbers twenty-three and twenty-eight.

For a long time, when he was younger, Freud was obsessed with the number fifty-one, believing it to be the age at which he would die. Later, after he surpassed that age, he became fond of sixty-two, as he saw it recur throughout his life through dates, phone numbers, hotel room numbers, and so on. In the end, neither one of those numbers was particularly meaningful. He died in 1939 at the age of eighty-three.

Scientists

The great Nobel prize winning physicist, **Neils Bohr,** from Copenhagen kept a horseshoe hanging on the wall over his desk.

Sports

Baseball:

Babe Ruth had to touch first base with his foot on the way to outfield.

Wade Boggs: Known as the "Chicken Man," Boggs would eat poultry before every game and was obsessively compulsive about his routine. Also before each at-bat, he would write the Hebrew word "Chai" meaning life, into the dirt of the batter's box.

Basketball:

Michael Jordan wore his North Carolina shorts under his Bulls uniform shorts every game.

Golf:

Jack Nicklaus must carry three pennies with him every time he plays golf.

Hockey:

Wayne Gretzky would never cut his hair before a game. He did once and his team lost that night.

The New York Islanders began the playoff beard superstition during their run for the Stanley Cup in the early 1980s. They won four cups in four years!

Ice Skating

Tai Babilonia always wears a gold crescent-moon pendant given to hear by Stevie Nicks in 1979. The one time she didn't wear it was before the short program at the Olympics and that says it all.

Brian Boitano always puts his left skate on first.

Oksana Baiul steps on the ice only with the left foot. She also always puts her guards next to each other on the boards, very close to each other and they have to be perfect. It is very bad luck if someone is touching them.

Racing:

Race-car driver **Rick Mears** refuses to allow peanuts near his car.

Soccer:

Brazilian player and coach **Mario Zagallo** is known for his unshakable faith in the number thirteen. Since Saint Anthony's Day is celebrated on the thirteenth of June, all things thirteen were preferred by Zagallo. He married on his patron saint's day, lived on the thirteenth floor, saw Brazil through thirteen World Cup victories and aided his post-op recovery from stomach cancer by visiting the saint's shrine all of thirteen times! **Les Bleus** were superstitious about goalkeeper **Fabien Barthez's** bald pate! During the 1998 World Cup, captain Laurent Blanc kissed the keeper on the head and France went on to win! With that, a ritual was born, with Barthez offering up his head for the habitual kiss before each match, often to the tune of Gloria Gaynor's 'I Will Survive,' which was blasted in the locker room to get them into winning mode!

Swimming

Michael Phelps, who has shattered world records, listens to his Rap music, removes his ear buds, takes off his jacket, climbs up on the block and flaps his arms like a gigantic bald eagle about to swoop down on prey.

Tennis:

Serena Williams will not change her socks once during a tournament. She only wears a single pair during an entire tournament.